The Dragon Bone

Journal

2024 ISSUE

The Dragon Bone Journal
2024 Issue

ISBN: 978-1-962337-00-7

Published in Hackett, Arkansas USA by Dragon Bone Publishing™ 2024.

Complied and edited by Effie Joe Stock
Reviewed by Nathaniel Luscombe
Front page designed by Effie Joe Stock

Trigger Warnings:

Mentions of death and scenes of death
Implied Suicide: The Last Rosefruit
Attempts to Raise the Dead: The Early Intrigue of Lia Grimsli

THE 2024 ISSUE

THE
DRAGON BONE
JOURNAL

COMPILED BY
EFFIE JOE STOCK

Escape With Us

Look no further for your next favorite book!

Our team can have a pretty hard time agreeing on the best books since we all have different tastes, but these top 3 books had all of our hearts from the very beginning to the very end.

Our Top Three Dragon Bone Approved Indie Books of 2023

It's hard for an adventurous comedy to tick all the boxes for action, serious stakes, and morality without seeming forced or cheesy, but

#1 Robbing Centaurs and Other Bad Ideas

Bethany Meyer has proven to be a storytelling genius who needs to be on your radar! RCOBI follows Archer and Wick, a pair of unlikely heroes who reeeaaalllly don't want to be there, and certainly not together. Their journey together is full of hilarious conversations and near-death experiences (and there's a WHAT in the bag???). Robbing Centaurs and Other Bad Ideas is definitely a must-read!

—*Abrigail Julian*

#2 The Planets We Become

Chaotic, heart wrenching, picturesque: The Planets We Become is a masterpiece to be devoured by anyone who longs to be a part of something greater than themselves, something that transcends time, and earthly limitations. Nathaniel Luscombe is no stranger to deep, rolling emotion that drives deep in the reader's heart and this novella is no exception. With sandy landscapes and advanced technology, mystery in the driving plot, and poetry in the words themselves, The Planets We Become brings a new twist to the sci-fi genre and won't be a story you easily forget.

—*Effie Joe Stock, Author of The Shadows of Light*

Heir of Two Kingdoms is the type of epic fantasy that deserves praise. Effie Joe Stock writes a complex, layered plot full of flawed, realistic characters. Her writing flows really well, matching the

#3 Heir of Two Kingdoms

pace perfectly. I could not get enough of this book. There were moments I had to put it down and process, unable to continue without letting what happened sink in. That's when you know a book is worth reading. Stephania is one of the most enjoyable main characters I've read. I can't wait to see where this series takes her.

—*Nathaniel Luscombe, author of Moon Soul*

Dragon Bone News

All the Exciting 2024 Updates for Dragon Bone Publishing

Dragon Bone Publishing was born out of a dream of passion. Passion for writing, reading, learning, and for life itself. Believing everything has a deeper meaning and complexity than often explored, Dragon Bone Publishing seeks to expose the depth and intricacy of the world around us using the words of multi-faceted authors, the magic and mystery of epic fantasy, the science and possibility of sci-fi, the symbolism and truths of allegory, and the wonder of a child's mind.

Submissions Are Open!

Want to be published by us? Submissions for anthologies and the Journal are open!

Our mission at Dragon Bone Publishing™ is to encourage authors with their passions by publishing their writing, offering tools and tricks of the trade, and by spreading the word about their work! What better way to do that than a magazine?

Want to get in on the action in the 2025 Issue of the Dragon Bone Journal?
Submissions open January 1st, 2024!
For more information and the submission form, visit:
www.dragonbonepublishing.com

The Dragon Bone Journal 2025 Issue

Visit   www.dragonbonepublishing.com for more info & the submission form.

Submissions Open February 1st, 2024

I Love You Unconventionally An Anthology on Unique Love

Where Aphotic Love was created to expose the darker, tragic side of love, I Love You Unconventionally is all about displaying the unique side of love, one that ranges past romance, reaching to also include platonic and familial love. We're looking to create an anthology that comforts readers, brings to light unusual examples of love, and renews hope in love, while also pushing the boundaries of what society wants us to think love is. I Love You Unconventionally is a book both tragically beautiful, and beautifully tragic.

This anthology will be broken up into three main categories: Familial, Platonic, and Romantic.
Short stories and poetry of all genres will be accepted as long as they fit the overall theme.

New Releases

All of our titles are available internationally, through our local distrubution channels and/or on our website www.dragonbonepublishing.com/shop

Turklet, Squeaky, and the Seven Chicken Chicks by Effie Joe Stock

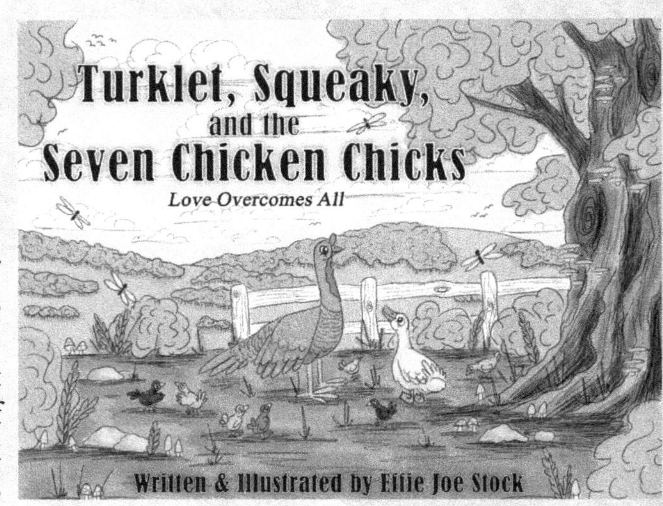

Turklet the turkey has always wanted a family of her own, but when she tries to hatch a nest of eggs, she is faced with many unforeseen difficulties including language barriers, adoption, racism, and prejudice against mixed/unconventional families. But with the help of Nic, the farm girl who raised her, and her dear friend Squeaky the duck, Turklet will discover that all of life's difficulties are not so daunting when dealt with patience and love.

Written and illustrated by Effie Joe Stock (the farm girl herself), and based on a true story, Turklet, Squeaky, and the Seven Chicken Chicks brings to light some of the hardships of families in a fun, gentle way that is sure to spark love and acceptance into the hearts of young and old readers alike.

Bleached Reminders by Effie Joe Stock

Sacrifice Rock-a place of grief, of loneliness, of tearful goodbyes as a girl lays to rest her deceased pets. But in a forest as quiet and gentle as this, is she really alone after all? Is it truly a place of goodbyes?

Bleached Reminders-left behind after death, often hated, precious memories left for those to come.

The Soul-Filled Skulls of Epsie Rees-a witch born to a coven intolerant of the magic-less. But she has a secret: she can see animal ghosts living in the skulls they once inhabited. But no one believes her. Will Epsie Rees find a way to prove to the coven that she is indeed a witch? Or will she and all her animal friends face certain doom?

A collection for lovers of both animals and bones, Bleached Reminders will leave you contemplating the finality of death while also comforted by the warm love of beloved animals.

Moon Soul
by Nathaniel Luscombe

"I don't think I can justify it any longer. I'm going to quit my job."
August has never been good with change and isn't sure who she is beyond her job of reading memories in the sand. When she comes to the conclusion that she has to quit her job, she's left with an overwhelming sense of emptiness. What follows is the quiet chaos of a girl regaining control over her life on a small desert moon.

Deciding to take a job in the hanging gardens of the Spire, August discovers more to life as she meets new friends, forms a different connection with her home, and faces an unexpected visitor from her past.

Rich in relatable emotions and experiences, inspiring in message, and written in prose that will hook you from page one, Moon Soul is a science fantasy novella unlike any you've read before. It will leave you feeling seen and understood.

Releases March, 2024

Human Scars on Planet Skin
by Nathaniel Luscombe &
Effie Joe Stock

Turr is fighting back for what was stolen from her: her body and her children living on it.
After the humans tried to colonize her, Turr was forced to resort to mass violence to reclaim her skin.
But in fleeing the planet of Turr, the humans left behind a chemical disaster—the dead zone.
To bring peace and life back to herself, Turr sends out a desperate plea to two shroom people: Invidia and Clyra. Invidia, though surrounded by death, is tasked with learning how to breathe life back into the land. Clyra must lead a group of broken failed experiments through the forest, following a trail of visions. Death and uncertainty face them at every turn, but only when they're all together can the planet truly begin to heal.

A science-fantasy like nothing you've ever read before, Human Scars on Planet Skin will leave you haunted by the stark realities of upsetting the balance of life, aching against the sorrow unmitigated death brings, and shivering against the horror of being trapped inside your own body. But more than anything, this novella will leave you comforted, knowing hope always exists in the life around us, no matter how dark our surroundings may seem.

Releases 2024

Short and Sweet

The Wanderer
by Jacob Mann

Jacob is never where he's supposed to be. His head is always off on some adventure, exploring a strange land, or meeting a creature that no one has ever seen. He always has a story to tell. He knows he'll never have enough paper.

Instagram: @jmmann_writing

He's a man that wanders through the pines. He has no planned route. He wanders from mountain to mountain, heartbreak to heartbreak, blunder to blunder. His mind keeps focused on the darkness and he keeps his heart in the pain. He'd rather have it feel pain than become numb.

He only pursues two things in life: God and the woods. God is the only one that listens to him. The woods provide him with the drive to live. God gives him the care and forgiveness he needs. The woods give him the love and beauty he deserves. They are the only ones that have seen him cry. They are the only ones who make him smile. He holds onto them the way bourbon holds onto a man's breath.

He inhales the morning mist with satisfaction; he smells the damp trees with joy. He watches the falling snow with amazement and he views the majestic mountains with intense appreciation. His heart beckons for the trees, the hills, the streams, and the lakes. His rambling feet start the trail without hesitation. He continues to wander, his only companions being the creatures of the land and a bottle of whiskey when he can fetch one.

He ain't so lonesome, as some people may believe. The sunrise gives him a warm hello; the stars tell him a lovely goodnight. He dances with the northern lights, the most beautiful partner that could be found. He roars at the bears and howls with the wolves. He tries to leave his sorrows behind. He gets away from the ones who have hurt him and the loves he has lost.

Somewhere deep down he may miss them, but he knows no one is missing him. He figures that if he can find no one who wants him, he'd rather be lonely on his own terms.

Isabel Harry is a fantasy writer dedicated to delivering readers compelling characters and richly developed worlds. Originally from London, she now spends her days ghostwriting, guest blogging, and polishing her debut fantasy novel. When she's not hard at work, she can be found traveling the globe in search of new inspiration.

The Tapestries We Weave
by Isabel Harry

Instagram: @isabel_writing

Dearest Reader,

Read these words and read them well, for they will be my last.

Poison carries in my blood, worming ever closer to my heart. My fingers seize and cramp, and my body quakes with the violence of an earth tremor. Through my shaking, I shall pen down what I know. If I do not, the information I have shall be lost with my death.

I never wanted to know such deadly things. You may scoff at my proclamation, for is it not an Oracle's purpose to know the unknown? I have spent my life learning futures, weaving them from whispers of thread in the minds of those I touch. The work I do is beautiful, but it is not what it once was.

Long ago, our kind was revered. We spoke futures at the right hand of kings and queens, but now we are but a party trick. Now we must sell our foretellings as if they are wares at a market. We defile the sacred practice of our ancestors by speaking falsely to our customers about the tapestries we weave. I see a man facing death at the hands of starvation, but I tell him that if he changes his job, he may change his fate. I tell him to return to me in due time to see if it worked, and so he does, with hope in his heart and a copper between his fingers.

But I know the future cannot be changed. There is no amending fate. The tapestry cannot be rewoven, despite what we Oracles may tell you. Our foretelling is a trade we must sell if only to keep ourselves alive. I separate myself from the plight of men, and I do not allow myself to worry over their futures. I do not design the tapestries; I only read them. I find no obligation to be honest to those I read for.

I had much the same attitude when the king came to town.

He travelled with a retinue bathed in majesty and grandeur, off to visit some far-off duke none in our town had ever heard of. His younger brother sat stoically at his side while King Torvin smiled and bid us good fortune. Their procession stopped with us for a meal and to rest their horses, and the king himself wandered about our town as one hadn't in centuries.

He regaled the townsfolk with colourful stories of his journey, delighting a barman by drinking his ale and a baker by eating her bread. Perhaps some drunkard had proffered my name to the King, or perhaps the king had ears attuned to the town gossip. I do not know. But an hour after his arrival, he came to me, a gold coin in hand, asking to know his future.

Men from his retinue bundled around him, his brother included, laughing sceptically to each other at the woman garbed in blue, sitting in a dark room lit only by candles. The king's smile was lax, his posture dismissive. He knew as well as I did that what I said was not always cohesive with what I saw. But I did not miss the severe glint in his eye nor the way he pressed the gold coin deep into my palm. It was as if he were trying to remind me how much he paid. He was paying for my honesty.

And so I removed my gloves, and I took his hands. They tremored with nervousness in my grip, imperceptible to those who did not touch him. With a borrowed nervousness of my own, I drifted my eyes closed and allowed myself access to his mind.

The seeds of his present spread themselves out before me like a field after planting. I saw the way he embraced his people, the way he revelled in their company as he travelled. I saw the stress he felt at facing the wayward duke at the end of his journey, but also his determination to bring a peaceful resolution to the issue. I saw his kind spirit, his grief at the loss of his parents, the way he fought with his brother, and his loneliness.

I took the threads of his life, and I began to weave. I would die for what I saw.

I saw a castle full of corpses slaughtered at the hands of those they trusted. A rebellion. An insurrection. The usurpation of the throne. I saw the king, a sword in his chest. There was blood gurgling from his mouth and pouring down his chin. I saw his brother standing over him, a savage smile on his face.

"You are a fool, Torvin,' he would say, 'your naivety befalls you. You trust they whom should not be trusted. You give to those below us as if they deserve the riches we have earnt. You walk the knife edge of diplomacy when you should be marching us to war! I will give the duke the reckoning you have denied us. Enjoy oblivion, brother, and know that none shall mourn you when you are in your grave."

I was thrown from the king's mind then, severed from his future. That was the moment he would die. My own body shook. I was rattled by the future I saw, more so than I ever had been. I could still taste the king's blood bubbling through my throat; I could still see the malicious glint of the king's brother's teeth as he smiled. Words eluded me. I looked upon the king and his men like a wild animal, eyes darting about them uncontrollably.

I could not help it. My eyes found the king's brother's, and they lingered there. I could not keep the fear from my gaze; I could not keep my knowledge from showing on my face.

"What did you see?" The king asked me, dread lining his features. In my peripheral, the king's brother disappeared, slipping through the crowd of men behind him.

I opened my mouth to speak my vision true. "I saw—I saw your death. You were—"

Before more words could find me, the king's brother was back, kneeling at my side with a canteen of water in his hands. "You seem startled, Oracle. You must drink some water."

"Yes, you must," the king agreed, and he took the water from his brother and offered it to me, a hint of shame in his eyes that he had not thought to offer it himself.

You must understand I was riven with shock and panic, plagued by the echoes of memory at seeing the king's death. My throat was dry, and I was still trembling with my fear. All logic had been driven from my mind. The canteen of water before me was just water, and it was held to me with such sincerity at the hands of my king.

I drank it.

I did not think for a second that it might have been poisoned. For all my foretelling of the future, I did not possess the foresight to know I had given my knowledge away to the king's brother and that he would kill me for it. Even through all the visions I had seen in my life, I did not understand the true malevolence of men and their ambitions.

I did not realise this until after the water had trickled down my throat and the poison had settled into my bloodstream. I did not realise this until my tongue became heavy in my mouth, and my limbs began to twitch. The change was immediate, and I was helpless to stop it.

Those around me believed I was having a fit brought upon me by my visions. They did not know much about Oracles; they did not know this was not a symptom of my gift. Very quickly, they sought to give me comfort. Strong hands brought me to my bed in the back room of my property and laid a blanket over me as I shivered. I tried to speak around my swollen mouth, but the king bid me to be quiet, telling me to rest and to share my tidings with him when I felt better.

His dread wafted from him like perfume, but in the end, he was just too kind. He would rather I rest and recover than learn what it was I had to say. He left me there alone, promising he would return soon, and I could only respond with a strangled squeak.

I know my death makes sense. The tapestry cannot be changed; I cannot live to tell of what I saw. I am not ready to die, but I must. The telling of my knowledge will bar the path to the future. It is a future I saw, so it must come to pass.

I do not know why I picked up the pen and paper beside my bed. I do not know why I wrote this letter. Perhaps, after all this time, I do not believe the tapestry is beyond changing. Perhaps it can be tweaked if only someone is willing to work the thread. I will be dead when the king returns, but my letter will be here.

My King, good luck.

Signed, the Oracle

Gale
by Sean Donovan

Instagram: @seanscribes

I wake up and there isn't any pressure in my chest. Before I went to sleep, it was as if I had a whole cinderblock caving my body in. I'm in a hospital bed, and there are two people next to me. Mom and Dad, they tell me, and they're somewhat familiar. There is another man, one in all black, in the doorway. He watches for a moment, and then leaves. They tell me my name is Kris. I don't remember having a name. I don't remember anything.

Mom and Dad give me time to myself so I can gather my thoughts when we arrive at the house—my home. They tell me to "just get a feel for things." I do the best I can in the early days. Walking is hard for a little bit as I have to adjust to not being in bed, because being in bed is all I've known. I look in the mirror, and I see someone that yearns for recognition yet is still a stranger. (Suggested: Stiches run up and down my chest) There are stitches running up and down my chest. I trace a finger over them and wonder why those are there. But I don't want to bother Mom and Dad about it. They tell me that, before I went to sleep, things weren't so great. Therefore, I shouldn't ask about it. I don't want to disappoint them, so I keep my thoughts to myself.

Once I'm fully back on my feet, they show me a bunch of new television shows and movies. They're…something. I ask if I've seen them before, and they say that I have and that I like them. I don't remember a thing about them, and even though I don't find much enjoyment in them, I watch nonetheless, and when my parents ask, agree that they are good. All the kids in these shows have friends. I ask about my own friends. Dad says that I used to have friends, but in the time since I went to sleep, they all went away. I can't say I miss my friends. I don't remember them. Besides, I have Mom and Dad. They tell me that they're all I need.

Mom buys me new clothes from the store. I haven't looked into my closet that much, since mom always says she needs to go through it and get rid of things. It's what I used to wear. However, the clothes she's buys me are…uncomfortable. She tells me that I love them a lot. She tells me to trust her as I wriggle into them, barely squeezing my neck through. I tell her that it's hard for me to breathe in them. She is offended, remarking that I don't trust her, so I tell her I do, and that the clothes are actually fine. Mom smiles while I resist the urge to scratch the itch the clothes give me all over. But I don't say anything because Mom is happy. She's crying. She says, "My little Kris. Just as I always wanted you."

The man in all black comes back about a week after I've woken up. My parents call him Mr. West. He lays me down in my bed and removes the stitches. He tells Mom and Dad, "Recovery is going well, the body is beyond the trauma stage. It's about time to get some activities in, just to see how the body will respond." Mom and Dad are nervous, which makes me nervous. The man in black also has a mask that covers his face, from nose to chin. Sometimes, in my nightmares, I imagine him with fangs, or a long, sharp nose.

It is strange to see Mr. West's car sitting in the driveway only a few days later, after he said he would be away for over a month. Mom and Dad wait for him anxiously in the driveway. I can't hear what they're talking about, but my parents are quivering. Mr. West looks through the glass door and sees me, so I flee to my room, to the toys that Mom and Dad bought me. They're okay as far as toys go. They're not…

They're not what I remember. And that surprises me. I remember the toys I once played with. I remember the story that I was telling with them, and I remember the pain in my chest I would feel when I hunched over in my room to pick them up. Mom and Dad didn't buy me these toys, other family or friends must've. I think they weren't happy when they saw me playing with them, but it's foggy. I had to hide them to protect them, and shortly after, I think, is when I went to sleep. Mom was shocked when I told her I know I have other toys. She said that it's impossible for this to be the case. I asked her for them, and she said,

"I'm telling you that you don't. I know you better than anyone. I am your mother, Kris. Why don't you trust your mommy?"

Shortly after, she told Dad that I was beginning to remember. He didn't talk to me. He called Mr. West right away.

And Mom is right. I need to trust my mommy. I wait until they come back from talking with Mr. West so I can apologize. I'll try not to remember things anymore. That'll make them happy.

But the next day, and in the days following, I do remember things. And I have to keep it a secret. For a little while, I write my memories down. I remember when I rode a bike for the first time. I remember when I ran around the playground across the street, the one I am not allowed to go to. There are bullies there, even though, when I look outside, I only see who, according to my memory, are friends. I remember asking to go to get fast-food and asking for ice-cream. I remember school and my teachers, even though Mom and Dad always fought with them about what I was learning and how I was learning. I find my old toys buried deep in my closet, and I hold onto them. I tell them their names, to let them know that I didn't forget. One day, we'll finish our story.

I watch more of what Mom and Dad show me while I think about what I would rather be doing. I eat the food they put in front of me, trying to taste, apparently, my favorite foods. Sometimes I lay awake at night and wonder if my old favorites are just something I made up. Mom and Dad are insistent on what I like and don't like, and what it is I want to do. I have two voices speaking at once: a combined voice of my parents, and my own. But my own voice is hardly recognizable. My own voice is in pain and wants to cry, but it can't, because then Mom and Dad will be mad at me for remembering things.

Dad catches me one day, when I'm outside, as I start climbing the tree in the backyard. He yanks me down and holds onto my shirt tightly. It hurts. He says, "Kris, what are you doing? You don't do that." And I let slip out that I always loved to do it before I went to sleep. His face turns red, and he brings me inside. He puts me in my room, insisting that I've never done that, never acted like this, and that I really don't want to even if some voice in my head says so. "You've always listened to us. Do you understand me? We know what's good for you. You don't. You're just a child."

I don't remember disobeying them about this, because I didn't think there was a rule about tree-climbing. But I nod, and I agree. Dad is upset. I don't like that. I need to stop.

Yet, I can't. I cry more often, in private, when I do things that I'm not supposed to. Even though I put on a forced smile, I don't like to do what my parents say I do. Sometimes, when I don't know how to do these things, which they claim I enjoy or have done before I went to sleep, I excuse myself to my room, and I do my best to imagine a time where I did those things. I never can. They get me to fish in the pond behind our house and tell me it's fun. They sit me in front of class work that teaches me things differently from what I learned in school and call it fact. And they are right. I know they are right. But I don't believe that they are.

They promise me that I'll be allowed out of the house one day to visit my family so they can see how well I'm doing. First, though, I have to continue doing well in the lessons they give me. I have to watch more of their shows—my favorite shows. I need to become more of Kris. Even though, if they saw my memory journal, they would know that Kris is back! I start to wonder if they ever knew Kris. Ever knew me.

Mr. West continues to visit. His visits are aggressive. He tests me with new questions every time. I have to force the answers out. I'm lying when I give them. Sometimes, I have to state a historical fact I know is false. Sometimes, I have to deny the activities I enjoy doing, and say I don't like my favorite clothes, that I think I look silly and inappropriate in them.

But, in my quiet moments, I can't ignore what is in my heart. I can't ignore the things that I like, the things that I do, the things that, I'm sure, everyone would say make me Kris. Except I don't have everyone. I only have my parents.

And so I ask Mom and Dad one night at dinner about these feelings and thoughts of what my life was before going to sleep. They are worried at first. Their worries aren't settled when I mention that I'm only curious about it. I ask if I was disobedient or a bad kid, or if I was just being myself. Mom tries to gently tell me, "You were never like that, Kris. You aren't like that." I ask if it's because of my missing memories. Dad tells me, "No. Whatever you're remembering or thinking about are just impulses. Ideas. They aren't really memories, Kris." Mom chimes in again, "It's an after-effect of the procedure. You were…asleep…for a little while, Kris. Things take time to get sorted out. We're here to help you."

After dinner, they show me photo albums. They don't have much in them. In most, I am a baby, and my parents are happy. As I grow older, there are fewer photos, and they are not happy. But I am.

I don't tell them that I remember some of these photos. They stop right around the time when I was eight years old, right around the time I went to sleep. I look paler now. But there is a brand-new photo album of me, starting after I woke up, doing things with my mom and dad.

"Look how much fun you're having here," Mom says, pointing to a picture where I'm wearing an uncomfortable outfit while holding a dead fish in hand. In this picture, my parents are smiling. But I am not.

Mom and Dad direct me to not reflect on things like my identity or my personality, since it's scary and overwhelming. I need to put my faith in them and who they see me as. I need to trust them. Yet I can tell they know I don't.

I struggle to show the Kris they ask for. I eat meals they want me to enjoy slower. I stretch out my clothes or change how I wear them. I think I'm being clever or subtle about it. Neither of them scold me with their mouths, but with their eyes of ice.

As another few weeks wear on, they become distant, as if they don't know me. They don't call me "my baby" anymore. They call me Kris as if they're being forced to, as if someone is pulling the word out of their mouth like a tooth.

I apologize to the toys in my closet's depths that they may never get to come out to play. I assure them that when I grow up, I'll bring them with me. I make sure to say their names and share my favorite memories with them. If I can remember them, they'll still be alive with me. Soon, we'll play together again.

Mr. West comes to the house abruptly and gives me a test. It's a tricky one; one that, I realize too late, relies on memories from before I went to sleep, when I was always in pain, when my parents were always sad. Afterwards, he returns to his car and retrieves an empty suitcase. He hands it to Mom and Dad, sends them to my room, and says they are to call me, "Gale."

"The resurrection failed," he tells them as my mom is in tears. My dad shouts at him. Mr. West puts his hands up. "There is too much of what was leftover. I could not make your Kris. I'm sorry."

Couldn't make Kris?

But I'm right here.

The three of them go through my clothes and take clothes from before I went to sleep, they grab a toothbrush and toothpaste. I scramble for my toys. He pulls me away, dragging me screaming out of the house—my home.

"Come on, Gale," Mr. West says.

But that's not my name. I'm Kris. I shout for my toys, but Mr. West says they can't belong to me. They once belonged to Kris, for better or worse. Tears stream down my face.

I look to my parents. They turn away.

"I'm sorry for your loss," Mr. West says as he slams the car shut in my face. "I thought I could deliver him to you. Clearly, our program needs some revisiting."

"We knew it was a risk," Mom says. "It's just…I can't recognize this child."

"That's not our child," Dad says. "Our child would listen to us. Love us. Respect us."

I did. I tell them over and over that I did.

"Then why couldn't you be the child we wanted?" Mom asks, her voice muffled from the other side of the window. "Why did you…turn against us?"

My father can't even share another word with me. Mr. West drives away from my house, with all my favorite things. Everything is numb. The world is a blur. The pain in my chest is back, but it is different. This hurts more. I yearn for the sleep that stole my memories.

At the orphanage, I wonder how I didn't listen, or love, or respect them. I was just myself. All of my things will be gone, soon, and part of me wants to smile that other children will get to play with my toys and have their own stories. Yet, I'll never see them again.

I wonder why Kris wasn't good enough, and wait in hope that, maybe, for another family, Gale will be.

Effie Joe Stock is the head of Dragon Bone Publishing and author of the Shadows of Light Series. She enjoys chasing all the experiences life has to offer while also dedicating time to honing her writing craft, and looks forward to watching Dragon Bone Publishing grow into a successful press.

Letter of the Infinite Walker by Effie Joe Stock

Instagram: @effie.joe.stock.author
Website: www.effiejoestock.com

To My Dear, Finite Star Gazer,

I'm not sure where to start. These last seventy years have been the best of my life. Anything else before it was meaningless. Nothing really started until I met you. But now that has come to an end. What do I tell you? How do I make you understand? I've held much back from you, but now it is time for you to know everything. For you to join me in the stars, in the dimensions you thought you would never be able to traverse.

So, I suppose I shall start at the very beginning, where all things truly start.

I don't remember when I began my walk. It was ages and eons ago, before many of the creatures that live in the universe were even conceived. I only remember a distant haze, like the sparkling of starlight when it is brightest in the dark just before a sun rise, and then movement as I began to travel from star to planet, to moon, and then to another galaxy.

Through my travels, I watched finite beings unlike myself rise from the dredges of planet mud or from compressed star dust. I watched as even other finite creatures were formed, fashioned from the same mud or stars, but by creatures infinite like myself: creatures who wanted something to rule over, something to amuse themselves with, or even something to love. The creatures they made called them gods.

But creating my own creatures and world to rule over wasn't for me. Mostly, it was just the thought of being tied to one place that I despised, not the idea of companionship. So sometimes I would stand nearby and watch another infinite and their creation and let a few centuries go past, but sooner or later I would grow restless and begin my long walk again.

Sometimes the walk was dull. It's unfathomable, even for a creature like me, how expansive this universe is. I don't think I've ever walked in circles, ever gone to the same place twice. Or even if I did, it had been so long since the last visit, everything had completely changed, and it couldn't be counted as the same. Maybe the universe it just one big loop, like you theorized.

Sometimes the walk was exciting, like when I get to watch a new star be born, or when one dies. I've watched the greatest battles of history take place, watched entire races and planets rise into the light and then fall back into the darkness.

But after so long, my walk slowed. No matter how far I walked, I couldn't escape the laws, the confines of this universe. As expansive as it was, nothing was new any longer. I had seen every pattern any infinite or finite being could come up with. I even came across other wanderers like myself, though I could never bring myself to stay with them long. I think we were all looking for the same thing, but it wasn't each other.

The end of my walk brought me to a quiet galaxy I think you call the Milky Way. Shockingly, only one planet in your solar system is inhabited, the one you call earth. It was just beginning its life but already your kind debated their origins, and how long they had existed.

Everything here was the same as thousands of places before it and before them. I would've passed on and continued my walk without a second glance this way had I not been so tired. So instead, I decided to settle down on the moon around your earth, nestle my head in my hands, and watch.

You've no idea how glad I am that I did.

As I waited, I drifted in and out of sleep, and for the first time since my walk began, I realized I wasn't as infinite as I had thought. The light inside me had started to burn out and I knew one day I would close my eyes and they would not open again.

I was closer to this sleep looking back now than I had realized at the time and it scares me to think what would have happened had I not gazed down upon you.

If there was a god above me, perhaps another infinite who had made me, I would've praised it for how beautiful you seemed to me. Not your looks, of course, I hardly noticed those since you were of something physical and I was not, but I could see the universe in your eyes, and I knew at once that in all my days of walking and wandering, this is what I had been looking for.

The stars reflected in your eyes in a way that I had never seen before. You saw them for what they were and more. You felt the connection with them like no one else had before you. The infiniteness of the universe made you feel small, but you loved knowing you were a part of something bigger. I saw the way you looked at everything I had grown tired of seeing, and I realized I not only wanted to feel that same awe, wonder, and love, but to cultivate it and watch it grow in you.

In a universe where infinites wanted to create, I simply wanted to love and adore. To appreciate something once in a universe where nothing was new or unique.

So, I did something I had never seen done before.

I remember the day I was born better than the day when my walk began. I don't suppose it was the same birth you humans experience, though. I was born all grown up; after all, it had only a matter of condensing my soul into the physical plane of your world. It turned out to be more difficult to stay confined in such a limiting body than I had anticipated, but when I shook your hand for the first time, heard your name on your lips and then mine right after, the hardship faded away into bliss.

Now that I look back, I understand so much more. The calling of your soul hadn't been something that had started the day you were conceived, interrupting my walk. It had been with me all along, dragging me to you, pulling me through the expanse of the universe. Your quiet little soul had been what caused my walk in the first place. Perhaps the dust of the star I was fashioned from had made you too. Maybe you were a piece of my soul I was meant to find and love.

And so, I did, for seventy glorious years.

I watched you grow in your love for the stars and discover things for your kind that no one ever had before. You made astonishing accomplishments, things that I had always known instinctually but got to discover again through the insatiable wonder inside you and the knowledge you called science.

Surprisingly, though your eyes were so much smaller than mine (you hadn't seen the endless things of the universe that I had), you seemed to understand the stars more deeply than me.

You explained to me that you lived in a three-dimensional world, that you could only exist in that dimension and understand that dimension. But you said there were other, higher dimensions. Ones that could see down on the lower ones and know all that happened, when it happened, and where, that nothing was impossible for them. You said they could move seamlessly across all time and space. Little did you know you spoke of the Infinite Walkers; you spoke of me.

Then you would open books your people called the Bible, the Greek Magical Papyri, and others, and you would read to me the verses that explained the demons, angels, deities, and gods. Though I never told you, they sounded exactly like the other infinite beings I had seen over my ageless walk.

In all the thousands of ages I had lived, that was the first time my existence ever made sense.

You made everything make sense, you, and that strange thing you called science. It was a beautiful thing. A thing where everything had meaning and purpose and understanding.

I loved listening to you talk about quantum physics, new telescopes that allowed you to see things with new detail: things I had seen a thousand times and never really cared to look at. You've no idea my joy when you would be talking to me, explaining everything you knew to me, and the debate led you to a new discovery, something you nor anyone else had ever thought of before. I had promised myself not to reveal any of my secrets to you until the right time so I wouldn't spoil the pureness of your discoveries, but somehow, being able to spark your genius and imagination made me feel as if everything I had ever experienced was for your enjoyment. And that alone was worth it all.

I know it's been strange for you to watch me remain ageless as you've grown old and frail, but I assure you this: you have always been as beautiful as the day I stared down at you from the moon and answered the call of your soul. It may be hard for you to understand what I truly am at first, but I think you've always known the truth in your heart. Even so, I had to write you this letter, to tell you for sure; I want you to know just how much you mean to me, not from an infinite to a finite, but from a creature who has seen it all, to the one who gave it all worth.

By the time you read this, I will have passed back into the stars to continue my walk again. I promise I won't wander far. I know your time is almost to a close. I will wait for you among the stars and will capture your soul as it departs for the darkness. I'll show you how to gather your energy and move among the stars. Then at least we will wander space and time together, across the bridges of the dimensions, never apart.

I will see it all again, and you will show me all its beauty and worth.

With all my love and infiniteness,

Your Infinite Walker

Live and Learn

Helpful Articles by Amatuer and Proffessional Writers

How Long Should It Take to Write a Book? By Effie Joe Stock

Effie Joe Stock is the head of Dragon Bone Publishing and author of the Shadows of Light Series. She enjoys chasing all the experiences life has to offer while also dedicating time to honing her writing craft, and looks forward to watching Dragon Bone Publishing grow into a successful press.

Instagram: @effie.joe.stock.author
Website: www.effiejoestock.com

If you've spent any amount of time in the #writersofinstagram community, you've probably seen a lot of posts about how to draft a book quickly, how to beat writing challenges like NaNoWriMo, increase daily word count, or other such posts. Or maybe you've spent some time wistfully looking after other authors who seem to churn out a dreamy number of books a year.

So how long should it take you to write a book? The short answer? However long it takes you. The long answer however is a bit more complicated ...

1. Emotional Capacity

Books are an art form, which means they take emotion to create. Sometimes we're in a good place emotionally and being able to feel empathetic toward our characters and write realistic emotions comes easily. Other times, it doesn't.

It's okay to be in a place where you're not emotionally capable of writing a lot. Writing can be healing, but it can also be draining. Sometimes the things we need to write for our audiences and our stories can be triggering for ourselves.

If you're in a place where you don't have a lot of emotional capacity, it's okay to take a break from writing, or to take it slow. Maybe even work on a different project. Your health comes first, your writing will naturally follow.

2. Genre

The hard truth is, some genres, styles, and age groups (YA, MG, etc.) take longer or shorter to write than others.

Epic fantasy sagas are going to take longer to write than a "hallmark" contemporary romance. Adult will take longer than Middle Grade. Even some books in the same genre will take longer to write. Epic fantasies will be lengthier than a comfort high/low fantasy.

Knowing your genre's general word count, how complicated you want your plot to be, and the reading comprehension level of your audience will help put a realistic timeline on your drafts.

3. Content

Regardless of genre, your book's content will affect how long it takes to write.

Keeping up with 4 main characters is going to take more time and energy than just 1. If you have books in a series, planning how the books will connect and plotting the overarching story will take longer than a stand-alone. Having one plot line with a few side plots won't take as long to write as several plot lines and dozens of side plots.

Other things like worldbuilding, language making, historical research, character design, and timeliness will also determine how long it takes for you to write.

If you have a complicated world and characters with a lot of worldbuilding, be excited that it's taking a while! It's supposed to.

4. Quality

Before I begin, I have to say, I don't want to give the impression I'm railing on authors who release a lot of books often, because I'm not, some authors have everything figured out and that's great!

BUT! If you're following an author who seems to release a lot of books in a short amount of time, and it can be discouraging when you're stuck on the same project.

Remember: any great work of art, or anything of quality, takes time to create. Editing, rewriting, reviewing, beta reading, drafting, etc. takes a LOT of time. Unfortunately, a lot of author who churn out books like rabbits are not publishing high quality works.

DO NOT COMPARE YOURSELF TO THEM.

Everyone is on a different path. They could never write what you're writing and vice versa.

Remember to spend time honing your craft.

The moral of the story is, writing a book should only take as long as it takes. I spent 2 years writing 800 pages of my epic fantasy and then another 5 years turning that first draft into three, then four, then six books and finally something I could start to publish. I also wrote 60k words in one month last year for a side WIP.

Not everything you write will take the same amount of time. You won't write like other authors. Some projects need more time and attention than others. What matters is that you do right by yourself and your project. Make sure you're healthy and you're putting the effort and time into your book that it deserves. The book will come. Remember to enjoy it in the meantime.

After learning the word 'author' at age five, young American writer Lauren D. Fulter has been captivated by the art of storytelling and the people roaming her mind. Though she longs for the cold, she lives in the desert with her large family, spending her days drawing, dabbling in the dimensions of the Fulterverse, and wearing sunglasses for unclarified reasons.

How to Balance Life and Writing Without Going Insane by Lauren D. Fulter

Instagram: @laurendfulter_author

I'm going to get so many words written after school! I told myself my senior year of high school, instead of paying attention in Physics class, scribbling down my plans for the evening in the margin of my notes. And maybe, I'll even draft an Instagram post or two! Dang. If I really push it, I might even get character art in there too!

Looking at my schedule, I was happy, inspired, and determined, thinking my afternoon would be full of productivity and prosperity as soon I get home—

—And then I fall asleep for 3 hours.

Dang it! Another day wasted!

There's a reason being an author is typically regarded as a full-time job. As any writer knows, it takes a lot of time and effort to literally craft an entire world, a fully fleshed out cast of characters, and an engaging story and then proceed to type it all out.

I started taking writing seriously when I was around thirteen years old, writing and publishing books in my series throughout high school. Something I'm frequently asked is how I balanced writing while being a full-time student.

The short answer is: I didn't.

Let me explain.

Highschool, college, or work (or even two at once!) are all emotionally and physically draining every day, unavoidable tasks most non super rich and famous writers have to deal with to a certain extent. Those in University are working toward a degree to get a job and pursue a career. Those at work are often paying for rent and the bills. Those in high school are…well, you kind of have to be there. Stay in school, kids. It's good for you.

Having life outside of writing is pretty much unavoidable, and too many writers seem to beat themselves up over this fact.

"I didn't reach my word count goal tonight!". "I'm going to have to delay publishing! Ugh, I'm so slow at this!"

I used to endure, and brave the late nights, thinking for some reason only getting 4 hours of sleep was better than failing NaNoWriMo.

While getting no sleep does help you crank out more words, it only burns you out in the long term. If you're not getting sleep, or making time to take care of yourself, you're only making it HARDER for you to be creative and to do your *life things* too.

"Okay, LDF. So, are you just saying it's pointless, and I should give up my hopes and dreams?"

No, sleep deprived writer, I'm saying there's a way to balance it in a healthy manner.

From my going on six years of writing AND doing school/work, I've realized my best writing and productivity often come when I'm at my healthiest. And when I'm at my healthiest, it often means setting priorities NOT checklists.

Here are some things that have helped me attain this over the years:

(1) Listen to what your body is telling you.

Sounds kinda weird but let me explain. If your body is telling you your all-nighter last night left you exhausted after a long day of work, it's your sign to sleep.

Writing while sleep deprived usually results in waking up the next morning to your characters transforming into fairy unicorns without you remembering.

(2) Discipline yourself.

While you SHOULD listen to what your body is telling you, you also shouldn't let your natural human instinct to slack off get the better of you.

If you're feeling physically fine, and have the time, you have to sit down and write. Even if it's only for 30 minutes before school. You'd be surprised how much you can get done in so little time and feeling great!

Sadly, since you don't have the luxury of writing full-time, you don't always get to write when inspired. Sometimes those words just have to come out when you need them to.

(3)   Set realistic goals.

I have vivid memories of sitting at a bench during lunch break my sophomore year, plotting out the perfect word count based on my availability that day (Approx. 1,500 words on school days, and a flexible 2,000 per weekend day). Both times I used that method, I actually won NaNoWriMo (in my sophomore and senior year of high school respectively)!

Setting word goals based on what's going on in your life helps you manage what you need to get done work/school wise while also feeling accomplished.

Setting realistic goals helps you feel less discouraged when you try to hit those extreme expectations, and often leads you to actually be MORE productive!

(4)   Consistency (and habit) is key.

Basically, all previous points come down to this one. Figuring out your routine, and how you work best is what will ultimately help you best realize how to organize your writing life alongside your "real life" one.

Writing every day (even if it's only 100 words!) is still progressing, and it keeps those creative juices flowing.

 You'd be surprised how many words you can get in during a 20-minute lunch break (I got to the point where I could crank out 500 words during my work break AND still eat…let's just say I've gotten a lot of questions from some curious Chick-Fil-A customers) or even in some extra time you have before school.

Relating to the previous point, find those times that work for you, and set your goals accordingly. It might take some trial and error, but you've got this!

All in all, remember that you and health come first! Being an author is *literally* a full-time job, and what you're doing is incredible. You're creating a story from your LITERAL BRAIN, and then WRITING IT DOWN…for OTHER PEOPLE to read!! That's amazing!

So, make sure to take care of your brain, and chase those words!

Professional Development as Writers
by Abrigail Julian

Instagram: @abrigailjulian
Website: : abrigailjulian.home.blog

Abrigail Julian is an author and musician with a passion for truth and teaching. She has been writing Christian fiction and nonfiction for as long as she can remember, and enjoys writing about Christian characters with real-world struggles. When she isn't writing, Abby can typically be found playing cello, teaching music, or spending time in her garden.

As writers, it's easy, even for us, to think we don't have a "real job," or that we really aren't professionals in our craft. It's easy for the only step we take in our career to be writing another book, or maybe working on a marketing campaign. But the truth of the matter is that writing is a career, a lifestyle, and no matter how much we work at it or read books on the craft, there's only so much we can learn alone.

Not every writer has writer friends nearby to go get a cup of tea and rant about the struggles of writers' block and editing woes. And many of us can't afford to go to these writing conferences that are championed as being so helpful for growing our knowledge and communities. So, what can we do? How can we still learn from and with others when our communities and budgets seem so small?

Technology has brought us far in this area. Social media connects us to other writers, and we can be intentional in reaching out and making those connections. Podcasts give us access to the wisdom of others, often for free, and we can share those with our online communities at the touch of a button. But we can be even more intentional and organized in how we pursue our writerly professional development.

For me, that meant organizing an in-person afternoon retreat with my writing group. For you, it might be an online group call via Zoom or Skype™ or maybe even FaceTime. You can choose many different routes for your retreat or conference, such as having members of the group present a topic, having a theme (self-publishing, marketing, writing craft, cover design, outlining methods, etc.), mixing learning with critique sessions, writing exercises, listen to podcasts on writing, reading aloud and having discussion… the possibilities are nearly endless!

The main things you need to know:

- **How many people will be attending?**

- **Where will the conference be held?**

- **What dates will everyone be able to commit to?**

- **How much total time will you plan for?**

- **What topics will you cover?**

- **What activities will you do as a group?**

- **What resources will you be using, and will any of them need to be paid for?**

- **Does there need to be a fee to attend?**

These are the general arrangements you will need to account for when creating your event. And if it seems like a lot, remember what it is: professional development for you and your writer friends. Get others involved in the planning process! Get their input. The entire event does not need to be on your shoulders, just keep it organized and communication lines open. But, if you want to take it on by yourself, take it one step at a time and don't rush yourself.

- **How many people will be attending?**

Knowing how many people will be at your event will help you know how much room you need at your venue (if in person), what platform to use (if online), how many supplies you need for activities, how much food/snacks/drinks you need, and how to divide costs if needed.

- **Where will the conference be held?**

If you're just having a few writer friends, someone's home might be a perfect solution for a private venue, or maybe even a local park or hangout spot if you don't need as much privacy. If your budget is a little bit bigger, or if you have more people attending, renting an Airbnb or hotel room, or even an event space like at a community building may be an option for you. Either way, make sure the volume level is appropriate for your needs, that you have space to do whatever activities you decide on, and that you have a backup plan just in case. Also, make sure your group is okay with the venue budget if they need to pitch in for that.

- ### What dates will everyone be able to commit to?

Dates! So important for obvious reasons. If you plan an event and no one can come, there's no point. Check with your people before setting a date. Try to have some backup dates in case something falls through or someone has something more important come up. The beauty of creating your own event is that you can adjust based on people's schedules to a certain point.

- ### How much total time will you plan for?

Will you be holding the event over an entire day? Or would your group prefer shorter amounts of time, but over a couple of afternoons? Or just an evening? Find out what your group's preferences are and plan accordingly. In planning around time, though, make sure you leave time for talking and visiting. If you overbook or tightly budget your time, you may run into issues as you have to decide between following the schedule and leaving in flex time to spend with your friends. The flex time will happen regardless of if you plan for it, so go ahead and plan for it.

- ### What topics will you cover?

As mentioned previously, creating a themed event could be a way of deciding what topics to cover, or you could do a mixture of topics that members can relate to. Receiving feedback from your group members will be crucial in this part of the planning process. Find out what areas the group members want to learn about and pick the most common topics. Depending on how long your event will be, you may be able to cover more topics or fewer. Don't overcrowd the topic pool. The more focused the event can be the better, but do what is right for your group.

- ### What activities will you do as a group?

Activities include anything the group will do, together or separate. These will generally fit into categories of either learning or applying. Learning would be activities like reading, listening to podcasts, doing presentations, and watching videos. Applying would include things like group discussions, writing sprints, and critique sessions. But don't be afraid to introduce some fun activities! Things like trivia games, puzzles, scavenger hunts and other games could be fun additions to your time together.

- ### What resources will you be using, and will any of them need to be paid for?

Many resources, like podcasts and blogs, can be used for free at your event, but others may need to be paid for. For example, the American Christian Fiction Writers (ACFW) have a conference and will sell audio recordings of their sessions and panels from previous years. They cost money, but it's an available resource from a reputable conference. Podcasts are great for listening to as a group, just like a lecture. Blog posts can be read aloud or read individually for group discussion. Books can be used for quotes, principles, story prompts, analysis and discussion, and many other applications depending on the books used. The main thing is to be creative and pay attention to what your group enjoys.

Also, if your event is in-person and you would like to provide things like notebooks, pens, books, or snacks for your group, these may also need to be taken into consideration for the budget. Don't forget the little things. Another resource that could fit into this category would be an invitation or event schedule. This isn't necessary, but can provide a touch of order as well as novelty to your event. A free app like Canva is perfect for creating these documents.

- ### Does there need to be a fee to attend?

At this point, you should know any costs or at least cost areas that you need to create a budget for. If paid options are on the table for your group, find out what their individual budgets are before setting things in stone. You don't want each person paying more than they are comfortable with, and it's not generally a good idea to have everyone paying different amounts. Find a budget that works for everyone and stay within it unless you want to pick up a little extra yourself, like for snacks or goody bags. Your event doesn't have to be expensive in order to be excellent. The point is connection and learning together. Keep that in mind.

If you've gotten this far and still have no idea how to put everything together, have no fear. As I mentioned toward the beginning, I organized a simple afternoon retreat with my writing group using these main considerations as a guide. Use my experience as an example, not a template, of how to run an event:

For my event, I had 5 writer friends, and our retreat lasted around 5-6 hours over the course of a single afternoon. It was held at one of our homes, and we mainly used supplies we already had for activities, which included discussion based on the book, "The Irresistible Novel," puzzle working while listening to podcasts, and a fun writing-prompt sprint where we built on each other's stories until time was up, then read aloud the resulting hilarity. Our host kindly provided us with tea and snacks and the perfect soundtrack playlist in the background. I provided the activities and schedule for the day. There were no fees for the group and, while there were things I would do differently next time, it was an enjoyable experience that I learned a great deal from and would certainly repeat.

As you move forward in your writing career, don't hold yourself back because you can't afford that conference, or get discouraged because you don't have an in-person community. Your career is an investment, both for you and for your readers, so take the first step as a professional and reach out to others, make connections, and raise your career to new heights as you encourage yourself and others through learning, applying, and spending time together.

Effie Joe Stock is the head of Dragon Bone Publishing and author of the Shadows of Light Series. She enjoys chasing all the experiences life has to offer while also dedicating time to honing her writing craft, and looks forward to watching Dragon Bone Publishing grow into a successful press.

Battling Self-Doubt in Your Writting by Effie Joe Stock

Instagram: @effie.joe.stock.author
Website: www.effiejoestock.com

Every author, artist, musician etc. struggles with self-doubt and making the progress they want. Something about putting your soul, beliefs, and emotions into art which is then shown to other human beings can be nerve-wracking.

But most of the self-doubt we feel as creators... isn't valid.

As creators, we feel everything deeply and we want others to feel the same way we do about our craft. However, the doubt we feel over our worth is only something we do to protect ourselves from rejection, not because we are actually bad at what we do.

But let's talk about minimizing that doubt and how to make progress in light of it...

1. Understand It's Source

In order to minimize doubt, we need to understand its origins. Ask yourself questions like: "who supports me in my writing?" "Who doesn't?" "Who am I most comfortable sharing my work with?" "Who am I most scared to share my work with?" "What good/bad experiences have I had in response to my work?"

Sometimes when we start isolating incidents surrounding our work, we can begin to understand where our doubt has seeded and grown. And most often, we realize that the words of others have no real bearing on our creative worth.

2. Search Internally

If you're like me, you may come to realize some of your doubt comes from external sources like toxic friends (or someone else in your sphere of influence) but also like me, you may realize that their words were actually reinforcing negative paths which already existed in your own subconsciousness.

Have you ever randomly come up with an awesome idea in the shower? Or maybe in the middle of the night? That's your subconscious working for you. Sometimes it's helpful, but sometimes it's not.

Understanding your natural negative tendencies like imposter syndrome, perfectionism, self-depreciation etc. can help you take steps toward silencing the not so nice voices in your head.

3. Align Your Subconsciousness

After you've assessed your natural negative tendencies, you can begin to release your negative emotions and replace them with positivity.

Practice mindful meditations that involve positive thinking or dwelling on things that are uplifting, encouraging, and good.

Repeat truths to yourself like "I am worthy to be a creator." "No one else determines my creative worth." "I am a good artist/musician/writer." "I am not selfish for thinking these things, or for lifting myself up." "I can make progress in my craft, and I will."

These thoughts will empower your subconscious to feed you good thoughts and motivation that battles the doubt. Say these things to yourself every time you doubt yourself or before you sit down to create.

4. Respect Yourself

While you're realigning your subconsciousness (which takes time, patience, and compassion for yourself), begin to respect yourself the way you want others to respect you.

Does it bother you when someone interrupts you while you work? You should feel the same way about interrupting yourself. Do you hate it when other people diminish the amount of work you're accomplishing? Then don't diminish yourself.

Make small, consistent manageable goals that INCLUDE resting and having fun like working on side projects.

Don't work on something you don't believe in or enjoy. Even if you've spent years on a project, if it's dragging you down, you're not making the progress you want, or you just can't seem to make it work, respect your time and energy enough to move on. If it's important, you can always come back. If it's not, you'll never regret letting go.

5. Practice

Writing/creating is different than things like math/logic right? Wrong.

Creation and logic are both brain functions. They both require the use of a physical muscle in your body. Your productivity, creative worth, and your creative quality is not dependent on born skill, a talent fairy, or random chance.

You can practice your creative craft and you can improve. It is as assured as practicing math, science, or anything else that requires the opposite brain function of logic.

Write a little every moment you can. Write poetry, short stories, journal entries, or blog posts you'll never post. Write in a different POV than you're used to. Write a different genre. Try something new and watch how you'll grow and change. You might even find something that works better for you than what you were doing previously.

Eventually your confidence will grow as your skill set increases. Don't treat your creativity as random chance.

Hone it and own it.

Moral of the Story

Most of the doubt we experience in creating (which can cause a lack of progress) is not rooted in facts. It is something we use to protect ourselves from creating and sharing and the POSSIBILITY of failure and rejection. After all, you can't fail if you never start. But neither can you succeed.

If you are a creator of some sort and have a passion, resign yourself to knowing that. Resign yourself to the idea that as long as you are doing what you love, you cannot fail, and every small amount of progress is precious. No one else can change that, not even the negativity inside you.

Start validating yourself and your journey. Empower your subconscious mind to work with you instead of against you.

Your art can only be made by you, and that art can change the world. But in order to truly change the world with your art, you must first change yourself.

Publishing Check List!

Think you're ready to indie publish your book? Let's find out!

1) Edit your manuscript as many times as you can (while staying sane!)

2) Find a critique partner, or beta readers to do an initial read for any major problems or improvements. If you're not sure what to ask your beta readers or critique partners, you can do a quick google search for "Questions to Ask Beta Readers" and find lots of great lists.

3) Hire an editor. Even after your own edits and the input of beta readers, you'll still miss some problems only professional editors can pick up! Whether it's for plot, character, development, grammar, or sentence structure, an editor will take your book from feeling amateurish, to being professional.

4) Learn how to format books or hire a formatter. It's very important that you take this step BEFORE getting your book's cover since designers will need to know the spine thickness.

5) Design your cover or hire a designer. You can find hundreds of amazing artists/designers on Instagram or who are talented at covers. Just search: #bookcoverdesigner

6) Research the different distribution companies. Between KDP, Ingramspark, Barnes&Noble, BookBaby, BookVault and more, you'll have plenty of options for printing and distributing your book. Do your research to see which will work best for you.

7) Upload your files and choose a release day!

8) Plan your cover reveal and pre-orders announcement on the same day to maximize sales.

9) Market, market, market your book all the way until release day. Don't stop talking about it!

10) Celebrate on release day! You've just published a book!

Words From the Heart

"Poetry lifts the veil from the hidden beauty of the world, and makes familiar objects be as if they were not familiar."
— Percy Bysshe Shelley, from A Defence of Poetry and Other Essays.

Amongst the Graves by Harold Straugh

Harold is a self-plublished (up until now) author of seven books. He's a husband and a father of three, and loves anything horror related. Halloween is life.

Instagram: @haroldstraugh_author
Facebook: @haroldstraugh-author

Amongst the graves,

    They sleep and wait,

In their nightmares,

    Lies our fate.

Their bony fingers,

    Wait to grasp,

Anyone who,

    Walks on past.

To pull us down,

    As we kick and squirm.

Only to become the food,

    For the worms.

So please be weary,

    When walking through a cemetery.

Do become fear's slave,

    So you don't wind up,

Amongst the graves.

Arrow by Marion Cedar

I imagine a stifling heat

A rush of noise, but no thought

Suddenly an archer pulls an arrow to the string

It hooks strong

The fingers stretching it to a curve

Then they let go,

The arrow escapes

It flies and lands with a thud

On the red mark

My mind is set

Bullseye!

Marion always wanted to be a writer. At thirteen, she decided that she wanted to be a published author. While working on her books, she got into poetry and now publishing her first poem, Arrow. When she isn't writing, you can find her practicing ballroom dancing, painting, or riding her dirt bike.

Lost and Forgotten Dreams
by ShastaJazz

Lost and forgotten dreams,
Stand huddled in the snow
Longing for a home.
Souls of those who wander here.

The son whose father is never home.
The child who lost all hope,
Moved too many times to have a holding link.
The daughter whose mother was taken away,
For unknown reason is no longer here.
The father whose daughter is far away from home,
Looking for a way to say,
"I'm sorry I was wrong".
The mother who lays holding the child
That fought for so long but breaths no more.
The unborn who doesn't get the chance,
To make a choice,
To make a life,
Or know her mothers face.
The mother who can not stand alone
And makes the hard choice to let him go,
And let him live
To be someone she'll never know.

Someone,
Sometime,
Somehow,
Will find these
Lost and forgotten dreams.
Take them home,
Build them up.
Be the father to the fatherless,
The holding link for the lost soul,
The mother to the one who has lost,

To be the one who guides the child home.
To show the one
Who has lost a young,
That there are others
In need of a loving home and heart.
To be the one who was meant to die,
But survived,
And now may forgive
for the ones who have died.
To be the one who takes the hero in,
Raise him up to lead his people home
For the mother who could not stand alone.

ShastaJazz is a stay home mom of three. She loves to write and spend time with her husband and puppy. She hopes to provide young people with faith to believe and trust the Lord.
To follow ShastaJazz's writing journey and adventures at home, check out DragonOdyssey and ShastaJazz on Instagram.

My Sky
by Autumn Floyd

My sky, my world, my light. Love like water, gentle waves. Gentle breeze, her hair shifts slightly onto her face.

A moment in time, with friendships short-lived. Something just not quite right, a heart full of love always broken. Words in her mind never spoken, her thoughts locked away, never reopened.

The sun setting low, to the sound of uncontrollable laughter. A life spent focused on subtle tastes of freedom and adventure.

Hi there! My name is Autumn, and I'm an artist, photographer, and writer from Fort Smith, Arkansas. I currently work in copywriting and social media, and I would eventually like to publish my own poetry book. My two favorite art styles are line art and textured painting.

Instagram: @Autumnowenonline

Muse
by Anne J. Hill

"Oh, sweet muse, hear my cry
Grant me inspirations this day
This book desperately needs done
So, lead me on my way."

Though the writer knew not
That he was actually quite near
And the kind muse she spoke to
Had freckled skin and pointy ears

On her shoulder he sat
Muse, rather proud of himself
She was his author
And he was her elf

He patted her head
And whispered in her ear
All the wonderful ideas
She needed to hear

You see, Muse was picked
Just for her by his kind
One elf for one year
With a writer in mind

So proudly he sat
Watching her type away
And the joy in her eyes
Made his tiny heart sway

Little Muse grew content
His eyes drifting closed
And atop her shoulder there
He started to doze

When he finally awoke, he saw
She'd closed her writing docs
And on the couch now she lay
Watching the magical box

But worst of all were the trolls
Dancing on her head with delight
Muse curtly pulled his bow
And marched toward the sorry
sight

He lifted arrow to string
"Who are you?" he begged
"Leave her alone, or
To the dogs you'll be fed."

"I am Net," said one troll
As he laughed and sneered
"And I am Flix,"
The other one jeered

Muse shook his head in fury
"She needs real rest!
Don't you see the way
You both are making her
stressed?"

"The magical box is rest,"
Flix said in fiendish wile
"Might even give an idea,"
Net sang with mischief in his smile

Muse had enough of that
And rang his arrow true
A warning shot indeed
It zipped between the two

"Yes, it can be rest
But not the kind she needs
At the moment, at least
And not with your crazy deeds."

The Fairies of Rest
Through the window they flew
With wonder and grace
As if summoned on cue

"Ah, at last! Save our author,"
Muse pled on his knees
The fairies scooped up those trolls
Tossing them to the trees

The little elf sighed
As his author stood to leave
And out the door she went
On a walk in the breeze

The fairies fluttered after
Helping her truly rest
Giving her mind a break

From epic tales and quests

Content again, Muse sat
Perched upon her shoulder top
Preparing for his next task
Collecting inspiration and thought

The trolls would soon come back
But for then, they stayed away
Bothering another helpless author
Until their return the following day

And every morning, Muse scolded
And fought with them all
Until the author's mind was taken
And someone would withdraw

Sometimes Muse rose victorious
The words written with determina-
tion
Or the Fairies of Rest did their best
To refocus her attention

Sometimes though, the trolls pre-
vailed
And then nothing got done
No real rest to be had
And all songs left unsung

But everyday, Muse stood fast
Against the trolls, Net and Flix
And magical boxes of different sizes
Nothing was too hard for him to fix

Anne J. Hill enjoys writing fantasy for all ages. She runs Twenty Hills Publishing with the help of her circus performing friend, Lara E. Madden. She spends her days dreaming up fantastical realms, researching ways to get away with murder...for writing, arguing over commas at the kitchen table, talking to the characters in her head, promising her housemate that she isn't crazy, and rearranging her personal library.

Instagram: @anne.j.hill.editing
Twitter: @AnneJHillAuthor
Website: www.annejhill.com

Children of the Innocent
by Sera Amoroso

Children of the innocent, engaging in the war
Players are the innocent, once they were, no more
Worlds that we have yet to conquer, let you be fore-
warned

Flowers, blood, river water, wash away with the flood
Players are the innocent, but innocence is mud; like
Children of the innocent, engaging in the war

Children of the conquest, be careful with your blows
Dogs are often parasites that let the anger flow
Worlds that we have yet to conquer, let you be fore-
warned

We are those who hide away, run from rivers to the sea
We are always there in the branches of the trees
Children of the innocent, engaging in the war

Cling to your mothers, beware of your daughters
We are the rage in the wind, in the corn
Worlds that we have yet to conquer, let you be fore-
warned

Direwolves and dying cattle, settle in the air
Everyone who shares your name, of them take extra care
These are the children of the innocent, engaging in the
war

Worlds that we have yet to conquer, let you be fore-
warned

Sera Amoroso has been writing stories since she was ten years old. Her debut novel, Torsion, was published when she was 16 years old.
Now, at 19, she continues to write YA science fiction and fantasy, goes to college for English and Linguistics, and works as an editor, beta reader, and book reviewer.

Instagram:@seraamoroso

I'm No Expert in Self-Love
But I'll Give it a Try
by Cailey Tarraine

When I wash my hands

grimace at the mirror

dust tiptoes down the sink

the pact in my palms reopen

with its exposed wounds

I whisper a prayer, and a pre-order

I'll buy beauty from myself

next time, when it rolls around

Labor before love

until they mean the same, soon

every inch of grime on me

will embrace my flesh

like I will with them

once they can be kept and sold

welcome, and so hard-earned.

Cailey Tin (she/her) is a southeast-Asian-based staff writer and podcast co-host at The Incandescent Review, columnist at Paper Crane Journal, and Incognito Press. Her work has been published in Fairfield Scribes, Alien Magazine, Cathartic Lit, and more. When not writing, she can be found reading about the global economy or shamelessly watching cartoons on Netflix with her dog.

Instagram @itscaileynotkylie.

"I dream and I dream
But deep down I believe,
I shall never be brave,
To do and say
All that I dream and I dream."

—Effie Joe Stock

Turning Legs Back to Wheels
by Effie Joe Stock

I woke again,
In a place I know too well.
I've wandered these halls before,
This place that feels like hell.

The walls here drip,
And the paint screams while it peels.
Glass doors on tired hinges,
Little carts with legs not wheels.

Dragging my feet,
I search for sanity but,
Only insecurities
Stare from sugar vanities.

A dear friend's hug
Warms my cold heart and whispers
Sweet nothings in my ears, that
Turn hazy in life's fissures.

Laughter hunts me,
Grating, growing loud and sweet,
Screaming with the paint, of things
I ignored and once thought weak.

For years I walked
Down these halls barely awake,
Hearing only that dear friend
Before realizing my mistake.

This is the truth:
The creature making walls drip
Was the one killing my dreams,
The friend always at my hip.

And now I know,
The laughter that hunted me,
Was the joy denied to me,
Not by sugar vanities.

But by myself.
I treaded near disaster,
To turn legs back to wheels, and
Again, I'm my own master.

I wander alone,
In this place I know too well.
In halls that no longer trap me,
I no longer live in hell.

Effie Joe Stock is the head of Dragon Bone Publishing and author of the Shadows of Light Series. She enjoys chasing all the experiences life has to offer while also dedicating time to honing her writing craft, and looks forward to watching Dragon Bone Publishing grow into a successful press.

Instagram: @effie.joe.stock.author
Website: www.effiejoestock.com

"Poetry is the journal of the sea animal living on land, wanting to fly in the air. Poetry is a search for syllables to shoot at the barriers of the unknown and the unknowable. Poetry is a phantom script telling how rainbows are made and why they go away."
— Carl Sandburg, from The Atlantic, March 1923.

Effie Joe Stock Interviews Nathaniel Luscombe on Why Short Stories are Important

Nathaneil Luscombe is an author, poety, publisher of anthologies, and writer of short stories and novellas such as Moon Soul. You can find him on Instagram: @hecticreadnglife

Q. Hello Nathaniel! I am so excited to be interviewing you today. You've accomplished quite a lot as a writer through the years. It's clear you have a particular fondness for short stories. Why do you write so many short stories and why do you think they're important for writers and readers?

A. If you were to ask me what my favourite thing to write is, I would not say short stories. While short stories have been a big part of my writing career, I much prefer to be working on a novella/novel. I used to only write short stories when I had a specific anthology that I was interested in. I thought that working on them otherwise was a big waste of time. I've since changed my opinion. I think short stories are the perfect writing tools for a couple reasons. The first is that it allows me to enter a world and try it out for a couple thousand words. I get to make characters and locations and decide if a longer story would work there. The second reason is that they're great practice. Within a couple thousand words, you get to write a full plot mountain. It's good to know how to do that. As a reader, I would say that they're a great introduction to new writers. When I read short stories, I often mark down the ones I liked the most and go find more things from that writer.

Q. I can see how writing short stories would be super helpful to writers in those ways. What inspired you to start publishing your own anthologies of other writers?

A. I found that there weren't enough anthologies looking for submissions. I'm very much a 'do it yourself' type of person, so I decided to run my own anthologies. I was and still am unqualified to be running anthologies on my own, but I had a lot of fun and released some cool (though under-edited) stories that I'm proud of. I got to meet a lot of amazing authors and expand my community. I think running anthologies and pulling writers together has played a big role in solidifying my spot among my peers.

Q. Building community among writers and readers is so beneficial and inspiring. What advice do you have to writers who want to write short stories and even submit to anthologies?

A. Don't let the fear of rejection stop you. I really struggled with my first anthology rejection. Up until that point, I'd never been rejected for my writing because I'd never tried to go anywhere with it. Rejection gives motivation for growth. Also realize that rejection doesn't mean you're not good. Your story just isn't what that particular anthology is looking for. There has to be a balance of taking critiques, but also knowing the strength of your own writing.

That is some excellent advice and something every writer should remember no matter what stage in their journey they are. Thank you so much for answering our questions today, Nathaniel, and we hope this has been helpful to anyone looking to submit to anthologies, or just start writing more short stories!

Cailey Tin Interviews Shanti Hershenson on Publishing Pressure, Overcoming Bullies, & More

A vivacious reader and spirited writer, Cailey Tin is a Philippine-based writing and spoken word manager at Incandescent Review, and columnist for Paper Crane Journal, Spiritus Mundi, and Incognito Press. When not editing poetry for the borderline or Sophon Lit, she's chipping away at pieces—some appearing in Eunoia Review, Ice Lolly Review, Sage Cigarettes, and elsewhere.

Instagram: @itscaileynotkylie.

In today's interview, I'm stoked to have Shanti Hershenson with me! Shanti is a teen author who has published twelve books, mostly science fiction novels, and a book told in poetry. We will discuss her creative writing process, how she overcame bullying by using writing as an outlet, becoming a social media star, marketing her own books, and making a name for herself in the publishing world. Being a teenager is tough, but she wrote around all of these obstacles and that inspires so aspiring young creators today.

Q. Shanti, thank you for taking the time to answer some burning questions. I've read that you're in the process of publishing your thirteenth book, entitled "The Bane of Angelfall Academy." Can you tell us about what it's about?

A. Sure! "The Bane of Angelfall Academy" follows a girl called Devan and her parents are both famous writers. She's sent to a futuristic boarding school for the most talented authors, because her parents help fund the school, and it's this nepotism thing. [Devan] loves to write, but with a lot of pressure to overcome, she feels like she's not good at it. Then suddenly, characters from her book bleed into her reality and beg her to finish her story. Now she has to deal with this, along with navigating the student body and the twists and turns of the school. When her characters come to life, Devan realizes that she has not only a novel to write, but a world to save.

Q. When you're writing these characters, how do you write real humans that feel alive and resonate with you?

A. Any character that is three dimensional doesn't exactly have to be well-rounded, but they need to have advantages and weaknesses, including positive and negative things about their personalities. I think we need to have their future in mind to shape these characters. Some of them have my feelings poured into them, but not all, because every character can't be like me. I enjoy using character sheets sometimes, because even if some [information] will not be in the book, at least we know things that can be brought up if needed.

Q. Most of your books are fantasy and science fiction, which is your favorite genre. What makes you love this genre more than others?

A. When I was a kid, I was introduced to many science fiction books. I loved the story of a cat who was a stowaway in space. The idea of technology and the future was something I was naturally drawn to. At an early age, I was introduced to Star Wars. My first books had robots that I loved. With fantasy, I enjoy exploring new worlds and escaping reality in any brand-new place.

Q. What was your favorite book that you wrote? Out of all the stories you've penned, have you ever gotten the feeling like, "if I could be known for any story, this is what I want to be known for," and why?

A. I have three books in mind. First would be The Bane of Angelfall Academy because of the plot points that were so difficult to tie together that I almost scrapped it, and I thought, "man, this is my worst book." But during the editing process, I grew a love towards it. Otherwise, Neverdying is probably the best book I've published. It was a breakthrough for me when my writing improved and so did my storytelling skills. It felt like it was written by an adult, and I thought, "did I actually write this? That's crazy!" The other book, not yet published, was what I wrote in winter, and I only have a few social media posts on it but it's so good, it'll probably come out in early 2024 because it's a super long one to edit.

Q. Your novel told in poetry, entitled "You Won't Know Her Name" perfectly shared your struggles with bullying, and it tells your real-life story as the victim of incredibly harsh bullying, which included sensitive topics. How does your poetry process differ from writing novels? Especially with difficult topics?

A. I did a thousand words of poetry every single day, which was about ten poems. They're in chronological order that explain what happened [in my experience.] Some are more poetic while others are rough, but that's okay, because the story is rough. That book was one of the hardest to write, not because the process was particularly challenging, nor because I struggled with writer's block, but I always woke up telling myself, "why are you writing this? This is a bad idea, just stop." That was my daily thought process, which was wrong.

Q. You're such a strong advocate of anti-bullying. How was writing something that guided you with life's challenges, as reflected in your poetry book?

A. Poetry, and specifically shorter stories have been an outlet for my emotions. I write about things that upset and scare me, it's a great way to lift a weight off of my chest, just getting it on paper. In the aftermath of being severely bullied, I really wanted to get the story out. I didn't want to keep in, writing was a way I could process things, maybe share it with other people. The situation was ridiculous and originally I wanted to write it as a novel, like a non-fiction of me going through the [bullying] events and sharing what I wish I could've said in those moments. I barely got through the second chapter. Another idea was a fiction, almost reminiscent story, and the other one was a standpoint of how I was surviving and coping afterwards. None of those ideas worked; my big problem was that I can't use anyone's names because I don't want to get sued, nor call people out. I didn't want to change the names because it felt less personal. In the end, I realized poetry is perfect because it's and it plays such a big role in my story, which was cool because it's about poetry and actually poetry.

Q. When I was checking out your other novels, what specifically stood out to me were the blurbs. Just how concise, well written, and closely woven to the story they are. When you're beginning your story, do you already have a blurb in mind? Or does it flow to you naturally, how do you navigate that?

A. Most of the time I don't write the blurb until the halfway mark, which I did with my first book, Biome Lock, when it was time to promote it. But it really depends on the book, whether they're challenging. Sometimes it takes multiple revisions and I let someone read through them. Other times it's a first draft, then I'll read it through and there is nothing to fix. With a few stories, my ideas completely change at the halfway mark. I have a weird writing process where sometimes I only know little plot points to piece together as the story goes on, then it slowly falls into place.

Q. What are some key aspects of storytelling that you really want to focus on in your work? Whether that be character development or plot points, what do you focus the most on?

A. I feel you can't have a good book without strong characters. It needs to be a character-driven story, I'm more of a character writer myself because I need to focus on their journeys. I love a strong plot, but the most underrated and overshadowed thing is the setting. I'm a sucker for vivid locations, and I strive to focus on it more.

Q. How do you balance relationships, school, and all these other things with your passion for writing?

A. I had to learn a ton of time management skills that I didn't have before. Thankfully, I'm allowed to write on my school computer during homeroom. I do as much writing as I need at home, then I'll do schoolwork. If I have lots of schoolwork, then I do thirty minutes of that and alternate it with writing. My goal is one thousand words a day, but lately I've been averaging two thousand words. Learning to switch from these two was a helpful, valuable skill.

Q. That sounds incredibly motivating. With all the passion you've been putting into writing, what was the exact moment where you felt like you wanted to be a writer?

A. In elementary school, I thought that writing books when I was older would be cool, but I wrote short stories then while thinking, "maybe when I'm an adult I could write a full-length novel." The time I discovered that I could make this a career as a teenager was in sixth grade, when I penned two novellas with a friend, and we self-published them through Amazon KDP. They didn't sell well, so I returned to short stories thinking, "I can't write a full book and become successful." But one day, my family and I were at the beach, it was getting dark, and I was wondering what to do because I was very bored. I thought of watching movies or playing video games, but it felt boring. I told my sister, "it would be cool to write a book and say that I made it, but what would I do though?" Then I got the idea of teenagers stuck in these biomes and they couldn't move, and over time, that became my current four books, one of the first in the series being Biome Lock. There was a crossover novel, so in total that would be five books.

Q. Who was your biggest inspiration when you began writing? Whether it be a popular author, famous person, close friend, anyone?

A. I always stop every time I get that question because it's changed so much. There are authors of the books I'm currently reading, but then that would be such a long list. One of my inspirations is my younger self, particularly in fourth grade, because I was always creating stories. I love the idea of my younger self seeing me now and going, "oh my gosh, we made it!" Funny enough, I'm currently working on a screenplay for school about a famous author who gets to meet her younger self.

Q. Let's talk about book publishing and marketing. It's filled with overwhelming things where we have to stop actually writing in order to market. Were there particular resources that helped you through it?

A. Sometimes marketing is harder than writing itself. When I began writing my book, I thought, "these have to be successful. As a teenager, I need to make a name for myself." I had moments where I'd stay up really late and wonder if my work would pay off one day. I read all these blog posts that gave me lists of markets before I needed them, and that was helpful. I began posting on TikTok, and it blew up for me. Editing Biome Lock was a challenging editing process, and during it, I ended up writing a series of novellas that got published before it. With those books, I experimented with marketing tactics as I did giveaways, and from there I kept going. Now I have a concrete plan on what gets sales, what doesn't, and the only way to make books successful is to keep trying new things.

Q. Sometimes the industry makes you want to focus on a specific type of book. How do you manage these expectations while still staying true to what you love writing?

A. If I'm writing something because other people want it, then it wouldn't be as great. Fan service is awesome and I like putting little things in my book that readers suggest, but only when I agree with it. People push for mature scenes in my books all the time, but I ignore it because it isn't my genuine work. I think people who write more mature books are cool, but I'm fifteen; I don't want adults to read books that don't stay true to my audience. Some reviewers go, "when is it gonna get spicy?" but it's a young adult novel and I also need to stay true to myself. There's a lot of pressure on authors to stay in one genre and stick to that, but I want to experiment with a variety of books, which means having more readers and reaching more people. I want to write books targeted to teens, then also kids, too.

Q. You've been consistent with social media posts, with over fifty thousand followers on TikTok. How do you continue doing something that can get extremely draining, and not letting it affect your mental health?

A. Tiktok is one of my biggest resources for marketing, but it's also a struggle. For every one hundred comments that are nice and supportive, there's a rude person. Although I don't get that many hate comments, occasionally some are pretty mean. There was an incident where someone uploaded my TikTok for free in a compilation with other TikTok videos related to books and writing, but they misspelled something in the caption and everyone thought it was me who wrote it. They absolutely came for me! Luckily that's all sorted out now.

Q. How do you convert negativity and experiences like this into art, and into your stories?

A. I remind myself that every successful writer faces criticism. In every book signing, there are questions asked [regarding] how to deal with negative reviews, and every author's answer varies. But for me, when the review is constructive, then I'll apply it to my next book and forget about the first, because it's already published after all. It's also important to remember that people like different things, and sometimes they're not even part of your target audience, so no book like yours would appeal to them. We have to focus on the positive people, and make their voices louder than the negative ones.

Q. Last question. This is such a cliché one, but seriously, what is the most valuable advice you could give another young, emerging author, specifically your younger self?

A. Okay, I can get pretty corny and cliché about this too. Don't let your age get in the way of your dreams. Don't join the military when you're ten years old, though! But for things like writing, you're never too young or old to create a book. When you're four, you can still scribble on paper, make a children's book. A lot of kids that are twelve, thirteen, fourteen, or fifteen, you start discovering what they want to do. Sadly, many of them are told that they're too young. But with enough practice, a thirteen-year-old can write better than an adult. A tip that goes along with this is try to write every day. If you miss one day or more, that's totally fine, but just attempt to. Forming a routine trains your brain and helps you get into the author habit. You're testing out new territory and improving with every passing sentence, so start early and be consistent.

Katie Marie is the author of Saving Zora and Master of the Desert You can find her on Instagram: @author.katiemarie

Effie Joe Stock Interviews Katie Marie on What It's Like to be a Pantser

Q. Hello Katie Marie! Super excited to be interviewing you today. Now you've been writing for quite some time and always opt out of plotting your stories before you write. When did you realize you're a pantster instead?

A. Hello! I was around twelve when I realized I was a pantser. I didn't know of the term yet, but I was going through this workbook where, by the end you'd have written a book in a year, but it had me outline and it just wasn't working. I couldn't think of what I wanted to happen in the book and lost interest because of the constant forcing myself to plot, so I dropped it. That's when I realized plotting/outlining wasn't for me.

Q. So now that you've embraced being a pantser, what does your writing progress look like as far as drafting, editing, and later publishing?

A. While I don't plot, I still have some idea of what the book is. I brainstorm the story, characters, and world just enough to begin drafting! Most of the time I don't know much about the MCs until I start writing, then add my discoveries of their personality, quirks, backstory, beliefs, family, etc to my notes document as they come to me. Same with the plot and world. My brain doesn't work with having set things to follow as it destroys my creativity, so during the beginning drafting stages I see how things turn out, then adjust my story from there. As far as actually writing goes, I'm usually making up the scene as I write, and sometimes each sentence is a discovery. The first draft is messy for me, as I often change things in the middle of the draft or have a more solid understanding of the characters and plot further in. Which editing me then must deal with. Each book is different, so my editing methods vary, but because my first draft is always super messy it usually takes many passes of developmental edits before I'm satisfied with the story, then I focus on sentence structure and line editing. My writing progress can be slow compared to others since I'm a pantser, and because of that I'm currently unable to publish a book a year like some, but every two years or so.

Q. That's definitely a much different process than I'm used to! What advice do you have for writers who think they might be pantsers, or who want to try pantsing?

A. I think something a lot of people misunderstand about pantsing is that you have zero idea about the plot and just write from nothing. While that may be true for some (every writer is different), my advice is to have the basis of your story down, even if it's a sentence/paragraph, or you're going to write in circles. You need to at least know some of the story, the setting, your main character, and what role they play in the plot. Everything else can be filled in as you go! My other piece of advice is to go with the flow. Your first draft is for YOUR eyes only. It's okay if it's messy, if the writing sounds terrible, if the conflict comes out cringy, if you go back and forth on details, if you put in placeholders for things because you don't know what it is/called yet, etc. None of that matters. The first draft is where you figure out the story, and the second, third, sixth, and so on draft is where you make it better and hone in on what your story is about. No matter how big or small, everything can be fixed during editing, so don't stress and just keep writing! Being a pantser may make you feel inferior to other writers (trust me, it's something I deal with too) but know that you're not alone and you're no less than plotters! God wired everyone's brains differently, so what works for them or even other pantsers might not for you, and that's okay! That's the beauty of writing, because you can do what works best for you and still produce a polished and amazing book by the end.

Thank you Katie Marie for sharing your process and your advice! I truly hope this interview has helped anyone who is, or is considering being, a pantser. And remember, writers, no matter what your process looks like, you are valid as a writer, your story deserves to be written, and you deserve to write it!

The Last Rosefruit
by Amelia Elizabeth Clawford

A. E. Clawford is a writer (obviously), which means she spends a considerable chunk of her time procrastinating from writing. She likes to think she is pretty funny, but sometimes she writes non-funny things, too—such as the short story featured here.

Instagram: @amelia.procrastiwrites.

Aliana turns it over in her hand, admiring the deep red of its skin. It's firm, it's ripe – it's perfect.

Fresh fruits are rare these days, and this is the rarest kind. Rosefruit, she calls them, because she doesn't know what they are really called, and anyway she likes the name Rose. She always thought if she had a daughter, she'd name her Rose.

She chuckles to herself. Isn't it funny that she named a fruit after a daughter she never had? No. Her laughter stops abruptly. No, it's really not funny. But laughter is better than sorrow, because it is so much shallower. Easier of a hole to climb back out of.

She shakes her head, and the thoughts wing themselves away like startled horseflies. Back to the matter at hand – or rather, in her hand. What should she do with the last rosefruit? She could eat it, of course. Probably the best answer, really. But once she eats it…it'll be gone. And then she will be hungry again, soon enough. And then, not long after, she herself will be consumed by the inevitable end facing them all.

No, she cannot eat it, she decides. The last rosefruit must serve a better purpose than merely letting her live a little longer.

She tucks it into the front pocket of her tattered dress, and resolutely sets off towards the next-closest house. Kettler will have a suggestion.

Dust billows at her feet as she treads the dead ground, and she thinks of how she misses the grasses that used to wave across the plains. There is too much dirt, now. The only thing to be seen other than dirt are the five or six crumbling hovels, standing here and there across the land like forlorn meerkats on guard duty.

She reaches the first one, and taps on the doorframe. There is no door.

A moment later, a man with a long, white beard ambles into the doorway, a smile twitching at his lips.

"Hello, Kettler," she says, without returning the smile.

"Hello, Aliana Murrissey," he answers. "What can I do for you?" He looks near starved, as she is. She wonders…she wonders if he is almost out of food, too.

She clears her throat, suddenly nervous. "Well," she begins, licking her cracked lips, "I was wondering – that is, I was wondering if you had any food left?"

He shakes his head sadly. "I'm afraid I just ran out last night. I'm so sorry;, I would give you some if I had any. You could ask if –"

"No." She shakes her head, drawing the rosefruit from her pocket. "I meant, I have some for you."

"What is it?"

"I call it a rosefruit."

He looks at the fruit for a long while. Then, slowly, he shakes his head.

"I don't want it," he says. "I won't be living much longer anyway. Let's take it to someone else."

She nods without a word. Perhaps it is terrible of her, but she is glad he refused. The thought of Kettler living on without her – it hurts a little too much.

Together, they make their way to the next house.

Two taps on the doorframe, and then pattering footsteps approach—with them, a woman in her mid-forties or so.

"Hello, Li," Kettler says.

"Hello, Kettler. Hello, Aliana Murrissey," Li answers. She wipes her hands on her apron, and they leave twin streaks of blood. Aliana wonders about it, but says nothing.

"Do you have any food?" Kettler asks. "Do you need food, I mean?"

Aliana draws the rosefruit from her pocket and holds it out.

Li's mouth turns up in a half-smile. "I'm afraid a little food won't save me." She looks both of them over. "You should keep it."

"No," Aliana answers softly. She doesn't feel like saying more.

"Well…" Li cranes her neck, looking over their shoulders at a house in the distance. "I think Dune and Clir are out of food, too. Maybe they'd like it."

Aliana nods, and the three of them take the short walk to the next home.

Dune and Clir shake their heads in response to Aliana, Li, and Kettler. They've been out of food for days, they say. No use taking the last bit of it now.

"Is it really the last bit?" Aliana asks quietly. She laughs to herself. Of course it is.

Dune shrugs. "Beats me."

"I haven't talked to Richard in days," Clir says slowly. She eyes the rosefruit and then quickly shakes her head. "Maybe he will want it?"

Richard lives a bit farther away, so it takes them several minutes to reach his shack. The five of them march up to his door, but he does not answer. They find him inside, dead.

Clir bites her lower lip, tears brimming in her eyes. "We forgot him."

"No," Aliana says. "We didn't mean to."

"But we still did," Li murmurs. "Has anyone talked to him these past days?"

All shake their heads.

Clir sobs into Dune's chest, and for a moment, the only sounds are her quiet cries and Dune's attempts at comfort.

"I don't want to be forgotten," Li whispers.

Kettler tries to smile at her. "We won't forget you, Li."

Aliana cannot imagine that is much comfort. Soon they will all be gone. Soon they will all be forgotten.

She pulls the rosefruit out of her pocket and turns it over in her hand. Perhaps it has no purpose, after all. It is nothing more than a mere fruit. Destined for impermanence.

"Come on," she says, jerking her head towards the doorway.

Clir looks up. "But–"

"There's nothing we can do for Richard."

Clir's head droops, but she nods, and the four follow Aliana outside – back to the never-ending expanse of dusty ground.

They sit down in a circle, legs crossed, faces sober.

"We'll share it," Aliana says, drawing the knife that hangs from her belt.

"Wait," Kettler says, before she can slice into the rosefruit. "Let's plant it instead."

Li frowns. "But we have no water."

"The fruit surrounding the seed will keep it nourished," Kettler suggests.

"Will it?" Clir asks as Dune gently reaches over to brush the last tear from her face.

"I don't really know," Kettler admits. "But if not, at least it will get a proper burial."

Funny again, that a fruit would get a burial when none of them could. Not even Richard; for all of them are too weak to carry him into a grave.

The dirt crumbles under Aliana's fingernails as she pries open the ground, coaxing from it a shallow grave. The others watch as she places the last rosefruit in the center of her little hole, and then covers it up again with the remaining dirt.

She sits back on her heels with her dusty hands resting in her lap and looks around at the others: Dune's stoic expression and Clir's tear-streaked cheeks, Li's tight smile and Kettler's soft one.

"One day," Aliana says, making her voice louder than she would otherwise like it to be, "there may be a tree that would not have been here, if not for us."

And there is. Long after their bones have been absorbed by the earth and their names have faded from any mortal tongue, their tree stands tall, holding its ruby fruits and emerald leaves out on strong branches. The last rosefruit lives on.

DID YOU KNOW?

'Bibliosma' is the word for loving the way books smell!

Daphne Paige has always loved writing; watching and learning from her mother, who's also a writer. The majority of her time spent writing, the breaks between stories makes her remember she has an actual life away from her characters. During those breaks, she loves to play video games, hangout with her various pets, and watch classic black and white films.

The Early Intrigue of Lia Gimsli
by Daphne Paige

Instagram: @daphne.paige.books
Website: popcorn-publishing.com

Lia Grimsli hurries behind her father: a tall, lean man with thinning white hair. His footsteps are loud on the marble flooring. The fluorescent lights dangling from the ceiling above them cloaks the entirety of the hallway in an obnoxious white.

Lia knows better than to ask her father where he's going. But by the dark leather notebook held tight against his side, she knows it's for one of his experiments. Experiments she's dreamt of witnessing, of taking part in. Her mother banned her from even speaking to Father about his work, calling it acts of the Devil, Witchcraft. Though Lia has always known that science is called by cruel, wrong terms. Science is what her father does. What he's renowned for.

Lia's lips tug into a rather maniacal smile, especially for a ten-year-old girl, knowing that her mother can't prevent her from following her father's footsteps any longer. Mother has gone away. One drop of nightshade and Lia's secured her place beside the fabled Doctor Grimsli.

Her father stops in front of a stark white door at the end of the hallway. He clears his throat, raises his hand to knock, and scowls as the door flies open before his knuckles even make contact. "Perkins." His tone is one of dismay. "I was told you wouldn't be assisting today."

Lia peeks around her father at the taller-than-most woman, hair as bright as blood, skin as pale as the walls around them. A pair of thick, red glasses sit perched on her angular nose, and her face twists with a matching scowl. "And I was told a different scientist was coming to take a look." Her brown eyes flit down and snag on her, one eyebrow raising of its own accord. "A child? You brought a child into a morgue?"

Father clears his throat again. "Lia wanted to see. Is that a problem, Perkins?" His voice begs her to challenge him, flaunting his superiority, his title of Ground-Breaking Scientist of the Year. A title rightfully given. Lia may not know what her father does, exactly, but she knows how genius he is.

Perkins swallows, casts a doubtful glance at the small girl half-hidden behind her father's legs, then steps aside. "Jane Doe is waiting on table three."

Father leads Lia into the room, stride as precise and confident as a practiced hand with a scalpel. He stops at the head of a metal table. The room smells distinctly clean, too clean, though there's an underlay of musk. Riper the closer Lia stands to the table. A table as tall as her, preventing her from seeing what has caught her father's attention.

"Bring her a chair," Father demands, not bothering to look up from the table. He brings the notebook up to his face, skimming through a few pages before producing a fountain pen from his jacket pocket.

"Are you sure?" Perkins hesitantly asks. With a stern glare from Father, she hurries to grab a chair from behind the desk at the far end of the smelly room. She brings it back to Lia, face ghostly-white as the little girl climbs onto it, finally getting a look at what has caught her father's intrigue.

Father passes the fountain pen and the notebook to Lia, whose eyes bore down on the lifeless body of a so-called Jane Doe. A white sheet covers her from her collar bone down. "Write down what I say. Got it, Lia?"

Father asks, calculating gaze now set on his daughter's soft features.

Lia pulls her eyes away from the body and to the notebook. Inked depictions of cuts and human organs, of the skeletal and muscular system sprawl across the pressed cream pages. Notes are written down in her father's hasty handwriting. She lifts the pen with a steady hand, flips the page until she finds a blank one, and waits eagerly for her father to begin.

He leans over the Jane Doe, tracing the faint cuts and scars on her face with his nearly-black eyes. "Jane Doe. Caucasian. Five foot three. Brown hair." He forces open her eyes. "Blue eyes." With a sniff, he determines, "twenty-four hours old." He takes a step back, tilts his head to the side. Lia can practically see the gears in his head turning, steam billowing from his ears. "Sheep will do. Living."

Lia, with eyebrows drawn and mouth curved downward, scrawls in looping letters everything her father has said. Though she doesn't understand much, she can feel the absolute brilliance weighed in her father's statements.

"Sheep? You tried pig last time. That didn't work. What makes you think a sheep will?" Perkins asks. Lia understands now why her father doesn't like this woman. She asks too many questions and judges every action he makes. She doesn't understand science. Not truly.

"If something doesn't work, Perkins," Father chides, "you try something else. One sheep. Young. The heartbeat has to be fast. I want it by morning. The cadaver can't wait much longer or it'll be far past time."

Perkins sighs and nods. "I'll alert you when the delivery arrives, then."

Lia and her father leave the stale scent of the morgue behind, footsteps paired on the floor and shadows drawn out in front of them as they reach the section where the fluorescents are behind them.

Finally, Father breaks the stretching silence. "Lia, do you know what my goal is?"

The little girl tilts her head up at her father. "Your goal?" she asks, voice squeaky with youth.

"Yes," he sighs, drawing in a sharp breath. "The one goal that all my research is driving me toward."

"What is it, Daddy?" Lia tries to quell her hunger for what he has to say. What does Father get up to, late at night, hunched over the bodies of dead women and requesting the delivery of live animals?

"To create an elixir for immortality," he says. Lia can hear the grin in his voice, the pride ending every syllable. "But first, we need to bring the dead back to life. Now don't we?" He winks down at his daughter. "I've tried every common animal with a big enough brain and heart to animate a human. None of them were a success. But I have a feeling about this one." He opens the metal doors leading to a dimly lit back-alley. Lia knows that if she follows the alley toward the main road, crosses the street and walks for two blocks, she'll arrive home–where her brother, Henry, is waiting.

"Let's just keep this between you and I," Father insists, taking the notebook from Lia's hands. "One day, my darling, this will be yours." He taps his index finger on the leather cover.

"Why won't it be Henry's too?"

Father shakes his head wearily. "Henry isn't like you and I. He resembles your mother more. He won't like what science requires."

"What does science require?" Lia asks.

Father stops in the eerie light of a lamppost and smiles. "Resilience, my darling."

"And do I have resilience, Daddy?" Lia asks, eyes wide like dinner plates.

Father stoops down, cups her chin, his black eyes meeting her own. "You're me. Small, female, youthful. But still me."

Lia beams at her father's appraisal. She wants to be like him more than anything. "Am I joining you tomorrow morning? I want to see if it works."

Father straightens back up, the lamplight casts a long shadow across his face. "Not this time. I have no doubt how ready you are for this, but I can't afford to have a distraction. Science is too precise." He catches her wilting expression and sighs. "But I'll be home, and you'll know if it worked just by looking at me."

The next day, her father's face is creased with a frown, disappointment written in the steep curve of his hunched form. He doesn't say much as he passes Lia, who is standing in the doorway to the dining room, eager for some explanation of what went wrong. What he does say, however, is: "We'll try again, my darling. Until it works."

The Pitifully Primitive Planet by D.A. Randall

D.A. Randall, ThrillerWriter, was raised on a steady diet of Batman, James Bond, Star Trek and Indiana Jones. He writes fantasy and action thrillers that read like blockbuster movies.

Website: www.RandallAllenDunn.com.

The jellyfish-like alien globules oozed menace as they oozed down the corridor of their poorly lit starship. Noobi accidentally oozed into the back of his commander, and they both jiggled to the floor awkwardly. "When will they improve the lighting in this corridor?" Noobi wondered, his thoughts transmitting telepathically through his upper antennae to the large commander, who did not care.

Commander Gloobi struggled to right himself once more. After doing so, he looked much the same as when he was lying on his side, owing to his oozing and indefinite form. "Just watch where you are sliding," he ordered the smaller globule.

"That is just my point. I can't!" Noobi complained through his wiggling antennae to Commander Gloobi, who still did not care.

"You are certain your scouting report is accurate?" Gloobi asked, changing the subject to something of importance.

"Of course," Noobi thought back with irritation. "You have already asked me 977 times."

"And now I have asked you 978 times!" Gloobi thought back with greater irritation. "I am about to communicate our battle plans to the Emperor! And misinformation makes him most irritable. Most irritable, indeed."

"My report will satisfy him fully, I assure you," Noobi answered, as they slithered like snails through the next passage, pushing through the gelatinous door that reshaped itself behind them with a rubbery snap after they entered. They continued to slide across the enormous floor within, where their entire legion of military advisors perched along the curved walls surrounding them, their antennae quaking with obvious impatience.

As Gloobi and Noobi glided quickly to the center of the oval court, a hush fell over the minds of the assembly. All eyes and antennae turned toward the front of the room, where a much larger gelatinous opening had started to quiver. Through it came a monstrously large, tar-colored creature – shaped with the same shapelessness as the other aliens but in monstrous proportion – and colored like tar. It burst through the gelatinous seal, letting it snap shut behind him as his antennae telepathically frowned at the crowd. The supreme leader, Emperor NoNo, had arrived.

"Now that's a dramatic entrance," Noobi thought aloud.

"Quiet!" Commander Gloobi thought louder.

The humungous Emperor NoNo ignored the mental outburst, choosing instead to ooze with dignity and grace toward the commander and his lead scout.

Gloobi and Noobi bowed in deference, by flattening themselves into puddles. Then they resumed their upright shape, wiggling in the customary salute. Emperor NoNo jiggled back at them as acknowledgment. Then he greeted each of them in turn, in their native language. "Glib Glob Gloobi! Nib Nob Noobi!"

"NaNaNa NoNo!" the two scouts answered, their bodies gyrating in an ecstatic salute.

Emperor NoNo regarded them both, satisfied with their jiggles of respect. "You have news to report?" he urged, communicating through his raised antennae.

"We would not be here otherwise," Noobi thought back. "Because that would be irritating."

"Silence!" Commander Gloobi ordered.

"Your report," Emperor NoNo urged.

Gloobi and Noobi rose proudly, sitting taller and sticking their bellies as far out as possible, as a sign of their superior intellect. "The planet's inhabitants are weak!" Gloobi responded, shaking his belly happily. "Feeble! Primitive!"

"They're stupid!" Noobi cut in, too excited to contain himself.

Emperor NoNo flashed angry antennae at Noobi, warning him not to interrupt. Noobi's form slunk down at the rebuke.

"They have no military capabilities of consequence," Gloobi went on. "They still use propulsion weapons, the fools! Nothing but guns and explosives. Dangerous, but hardly a threat."

"Hardly a threat to Commander NoNo and the mighty race of the Jiblets!" Noobi burst out again.

"Silence, you pile of goop!" Emperor NoNo's thoughts growled.

Gloobi and the commander stared angrily at Noobi, who nearly flattened himself to the floor.

Noobi deferred to his commander. "My apologies. You were saying."

Gloobi mentally cleared his throat for the others to sense, then continued. "The planet possesses various natural ores, many of which its inhabitants have not yet discovered. The imbeciles."

"Those moon-heads," Noobi thought quietly.

Gloobi sighed and went on, ignoring the uninvited thought. "The ores are buried beneath the planet's surface. Properly utilized, they will advance our armies beyond even that of the Arturi race."

Commander NoNo's outer skin sagged slightly with satisfaction. Over millennia, their race had conquered planets throughout the universe, growing in strength and numbers. But they had yet to halt the progress of their greatest interplanetary rivals, the Arturies, who – problematically – were also bent on intergalactic conquest. "To imagine," he thought to both of them. "That, once and for all, the Jiblets could block the Arturies." He wiggled his body in deep thought. Fearful of looking foolish, Gloobi and Noobi did the same. "What of the planet's inhabitants?" NoNo wondered.

"Insignificant," Gloobi assured him. "They are small and underdeveloped."

"Nothing like the power of the Jiblets!" Noobi exclaimed again.

"Shut up," NoNo ordered, still wiggling in thought. "Continue," he directed Gloobi.

Gloobi hummed a spiteful little victory song in his head for both of them to hear, before proceeding with his report, while Noobi grumbled to himself.

"The inhabitants – those fools! – would easily be defeated by the galaxy's weakest race. Their technological understanding is at an elementary level. They offer no benefit as slaves. I recommend obliteration."

"Destroy the morons!" Noobi burst out again.

Emperor NoNo cast a harsh glare at him, issuing a telepathic electrical burst from his antennae. Noobi's outer skin began to shrivel as he cried out in pain. The Emperor finally released him, watching Noobi struggle to compose himself and his wrinkled outer shell. "Keep your place," Emperor NoNo warned him. "Remember who wears the big antennae." He nodded again to Gloobi.

Gloobi smirked inwardly, allowing his smug thought to be outwardly perceived by everyone. "We can remove them from the planet's surface in a few short cycles, then mine their resources and establish a new outpost there. We will be well-situated! This is the only inhabited planet in this region!"

Emperor NoNo's jellyfish-shaped torso rose and fell again, exceedingly pleased. "And how shall we classify this new outpost?" he asked.

"If I may?" Noobi offered. The Emperor signaled his permission. "The planet's current inhabitants call it – EARTH." He looked about the great hall for some reaction, but there was none.

Emperor NoNo looked about the room as well, to determine why Noobi was looking about, but he found no reason. "Very well. Go occupy this 'Earth' and report back tomorrow after lunch."

"Yes, Emperor NoNo!" Gloobi said with a jiggly salute.

"Yes, Emperor NoNo!" Noobi agreed, jiggling in turn. "We will go now to destroy the planet of – EARTH."

The Emperor wrinkled his body in confusion. "Why do you keep saying the planet's name so dramatically, as if it is different from every other planet we have conquered?"

"I don't know," Noobi said. "I think it just has a nice ring to it. EARTH."

The Emperor continued to stare at Noobi as though he was out of his mind.

Gloobi would have agreed. "We are off now, Emperor NoNo."

"Yes," Noobi said. "Off to destroy – EARTH."

"Oh, shut up and get going," Gloobi thought impatiently.

The jellyfish-shaped cruiser shot away from the Jiblet destroyer, which continued orbiting the sun to hide its position from their targeted planet. The darting cruiser's rubbery supports trailed behind its bubble-shaped head, but they would soon spring out in all directions to land on the surface of the primitive planet called Earth. Similar cruisers waited alongside the destroyer, like giant boils across the smooth circular torso of a majestic whale. Once the great Emperor NoNo gave the order, the boils would erupt from the galactic whale and strafe the planet's surface. Gloobi grinned to himself, thinking that the result would be rather messy.

Noobi mentally agreed, grinning back. "They'll never know what obliterated them, those muffin-heads," he thought to Gloobi.

Standard attack procedure dictated a time of strategy for the commander, based on a final survey with his lead scout. Commander Gloobi would investigate the planet, approaching from its dark side, to confirm Noobi's information and plot a systematic assault. But according to Noobi's study, the planet's inhabitants were so primitive and helpless that the oncoming Jiblet invasion could not be classified as anything less than a slaughter.

"We may attack at their weakest points first," Noobi suggested, his thoughts penetrating the silence of space around them. "This will show you their inability to defend themselves. In the face of death or even harm, the inhabitants flee, hoping only to escape."

"You have seen this?" Commander Gloobi questioned, outraged. "You were to make no commitment of force! You are only a – !"

"Wubba Wubba!" Noobi burst.

The commander's antennae rose sharply with indignance. "How dare you curse at me?"

"I know my duties," Noobi snapped back telepathically, silencing any further hostile thoughts. "I merely observed their own violence against one another."

Gloobi communicated his bewilderment to the scout.

"They are not united," Noobi insisted. "So they remain in a backward state. They will not advance to any level of usefulness for several milennia. Their own people kill and steal from one another, each inhabitant living as a separate entity. Their regions are divided, and have waged war against one another."

"How is this possible?" Gloobi demanded, incredulous. "How can any race be so primitive?"

"They believe themselves to be independent and isolated, apart from the rest of the universe. They are not even aware that other planetary races exist. They know only themselves. Thus, they fight amongst themselves for dominance, to see who will rule the planet, or a certain portion of it."

Commander Gloobi stared back at the scout, dumbfounded. "We must accept your report as truth," he thought to Noobi. "But it is hard to imagine a planet so disorganized, so ignorant, that they cannot serve as proper slaves. To imagine a cannibalistic planet that actually destroys its own instead of uniting its military might to conquer other races? If you were not our most qualified scout, I would think you delusional."

Noobi extended his antennae in a show of submission. "I am the Jiblets' most reliable scout, and have provided full details on our new outpost. The planet of – EARTH."

Gloobi's entire form quivered with annoyance, then finally relented. "All right, I admit. That is fun to say." He bent toward Gloobi, their heads touching as they harmonized their thoughts. "EARRRRRTHH," they hummed inwardly, their antennae tingling with anticipation.

The blue ball, swirled with streaks of white, appeared before them.

"Good morning, Earth," Noobi thought happily. "The stars say 'hello.'"

"Quiet," Commander Gloobi ordered. "We must focus now."

Noobi made a rapid approach, so as to avoid any possible detection by their antiquated technology, and curved around to the dark side of the planet. Their cruiser broke through the planet's white fluffs of cloud and descended through the night sky.

Commander Gloobi's antennae sprang up, sensing the vibrations in the terrain below to gauge the size and shapes of the various mountains, valleys and plains. Their silent ship went unnoticed as it sliced through the air, soaring over broad fields of food being cultivated by the inhabitants, in strips of yellow, green and brown.

They continued on toward a poorly constructed dwelling, which Gloobi sensed was contrived from the bark of the inhabitants' trees and painted a bright red color.

"Yes," Noobi confirmed. "One of the inhabitants' dwellings. Isn't it remarkable?"

Gloobi did not answer back. He was too astounded by the planet's lack of development.

"And look at their crop field," Noobi added. "I cut circles in it, the shape of our cruisers, so we'll have a convenient parking space."

"Thank you. That's very considerate," Gloobi said, still marveling at the pathetic construction below.

As they veered toward the red-bark dwelling, a small piece of it – a makeshift door – swung open, and two creatures hurried out. "These must be the fearful inhabitants," Gloobi surmised.

Again, Noobi confirmed his thoughts. "Yes, those micro-brains."

The inhabitants – a tall thin figure with a wide piece of gathered straw on its head, and a shorter, stockier figure with greater energy, perhaps a youth – came running toward the cruiser. The tall figure had a long metal rod in his hand, apparently an oddly-shaped farming tool. The tall figure stopped suddenly and leaned back, putting one end of the metal rod near its head, resting it against himself.

Something exploded across the cruiser's frontal shield. "What on Jiblet --?!!" Gloobi sputtered.

Noobi communicated nothing but confusion. "I – I don't understand what happened," he said, as he forced the cruiser up into the air to avoid collision with the dwelling, having temporarily lost his perspective of the planet's surface.

The bubble-shaped cruiser curved through the clouds and arched down at the two creatures below once more. Commander Gloobi watched the inhabitants, his antennae rising to sense the presence of any other creatures forming an army nearby.

There was no one. The two creatures were alone. Noobi bore down on them with the cruiser.

"Now they will retreat," Noobi promised. "Just watch."

Gloobi did watch, but the creatures did not retreat. Gloobi sensed his scout's astonishment as the taller creature brought his metal rod up to his head once again and aimed it up at their ship.

A ringing sound was heard as pieces of hard material tore across the ship's outer hull.

"It's a gun!" Gloobi thought in alarm. "He's firing his weapon at us!"

"Their weapons are insignificant," Noobi insisted. "They are too weak to harm us. I have confirmed it."

"You have confirmed it," Gloobi sneered in disgust. "You claimed they were unaware of other races! You said they were like a nest of eggs ready to be plucked! But this creature knew! How much more of your information is faulty?!!"

"None! I – I can't explain this man's knowledge. Somehow he – he must have …"

"Known we were coming," the commander finished his unexpressed thought.

Noobi tried to imagine any way that the farmer could have been warned about the Jiblet attack. It was impossible.

Gloobi sensed his scout's struggling thoughts and knew he was now questioning his own report. "If this simple creature knows, the planet's leaders will be even more prepared! With weapons that your 'report' overlooked!"

"No need to panic!" Noobi insisted. "There must be some logical explanation."

"Yes!" Gloobi's antennae bellowed. "You are inept! That is the explanation! We will abort."

"No!" Noobi protested. "We need more space, and their atmosphere suits us. This planet is ripe for the taking!"

"We will look elsewhere, further on! This 'primitive planet' of yours is too hostile, too dangerous, and completely unpredictable! Who knows what might await us if we landed? We are returning home."

The decision was made. Noobi said nothing. The Jiblets were an impulsive race, prone to quick decisions and immediate action. But superiors were to be obeyed, with no questions asked.

The bubbling cruiser left Earth's atmosphere.

"Daddy!!"

"It's all right, Jimmy," Warren assured his son. "They're gone now. Maybe they'll even think twice before coming back, at least to this part."

"Lucky we knew 'bout 'em, huh, pa?" Jimmy said, trying to sound brave as he hugged his father to hide his tears.

"Yep," Warren answered. "You did a good thing telling me about the warning. We can just thank God for our modern technology. Saved our lives."

"Sure did."

"Don't know what would'a happened without the modern miracle of radio." Warren looked off toward the East. "Look, son. You can almost see the glow of the fires in New York City."

Behind them, in the house, the tall wooden box with round knobs and a curved top continued to speak. The thick-jowled man communicating through the device could not be seen, and had not yet been recognized by Warren or his eight-year old son. Even as the man revealed his identity, Warren and Jimmy remained unaware as they stood outside on the lawn.

"This is Orson Welles, ladies and gentlemen," the radio announcer said to the empty living room. "… out of character, to assure you that 'The War of the Worlds' has no further significance than as the holiday offering it was intended to be – the Mercury Theatre's own radio version of dressing up in a sheet and jumping out of a bush and saying, 'boo.'"

Outside, Warren drew his son close as they watched the clouds through which the alien craft had departed. "Yessir," Warren said, masking his own fear to comfort his son. "Them Martians sure picked the wrong night to invade this planet."

"You can never get a cup of tea large enough or a book long enough to suit me." – C.S. Lewis

"Because she loves writing so much, Jessica did her Master's in Chemistry and learned that writing lab reports is sometimes almost the same as coming up with fantasy stories. Her hometown is one of the most crime-ridden cities in Germany but also the biggest village on earth, so she had the pleasure to experience the best of both worlds. She currently lives in Stockholm, where she takes the ferry while working on her novel about an immortal who tries to solve a generational conflict on Earth."

A Song of Freedom
by Jessica Erdmann

Instagram: @book.of.jess

According to the villagers, Yvellios's pointy ears were a lot of things: horrendous, disgusting, a bad omen, as wicked as a witch's pinky, the reason for all the pigs to die during that one cold winter and for the skin tearing frost to cover the lands in the first place.

He got them from his father, as the adults said. What an odd present to give. Did his father know what a burden they were? Would he tell Yvellios if they ever met?

His mother, on the other hand, was a pure human. From the perfect wrinkles on her uneven skin to the roundness of her ears to the fragility of her existence, did nothing give any hint of strangeness. Oh, how lucky he considered her for it.

While the other children made sure Yvellios knew what his heritage meant, his mother made sure to erase those memories of fists about to crash onto his body, flying dirt and sometimes stones. She sang away the bruises and scratches. Even if only for a short time. A single chorus and the soft touch of her tender fingers on Yvellios's forehead replaced the fear and pain with only warmth.

They sang them together, and he sang them alone, but he especially remembered her songs at times he couldn't bear the ever-present urge to cut off the miserable long ends of his ears with one of the knives his father left behind, buried under rusted forks and spoons in the bottom of the kitchen shelf. What a suitable use they would find that way.

Eventually, Yvellios learned to cure wounds on his own. When he hummed or whispered the melodies, his mother's songs not only shielded his heart, but also sealed its fragile wall that was his skin.

That day, it began with a strong pull on his hair. Yvellios had never been one of the stronger ones and there was no point in fighting back, when all it would be good for was making things worse. So he tolerated all the bad words he would never even dream of saying. Accepted the punches. Took in the kicks. Eventually, they decided they were satisfied and let go of him. He knew their procedure.

Yvellios remained, lying on his side. With arms around his chest, he began to hum. Slow and quiet tones to soothe his heart. Hands caressing his skin in gentle strokes, until every layer of skin was restored and the brown-red dirt on his skin and the tousled hair were the only evidence left.

His hair was the longest then. A silken flood of white strands never to be worn in a bun or braid.

He wiped his sleeve's rough fabric over the wet skin under his eyes and stood up. Tiny branches on the forest floor pierced into the soles of his now bare feet. Slowly, he made his way home, with legs that laboriously carried the weight of a trembling body.

The moment he saw their small house's straw roof at the end of the road, Yvellios straightened his back and shoulders and made an effort of an upright gait, in case his mother would see him.

The healing spell she taught him was a simple one, which sealed wounds and got rid of cramps and required nothing but bare touch and a song. A quite basic spell. It was enough, though, to keep most attacks from his mother's knowledge.

He passed her flower beds, piled with every color imaginable. While he balanced on the small stones outlining the daffodils, he saw the door to their house wide open. The clanking of metal drowned out a wild discussion. Words which he could not make out. But he recognized his mother's voice. A high-pitched echo paired with the deep sound of something falling to the wooden floor. However, it was the cough followed by a soft whimper, which made his throat choke up.

Yvellios half-crouched on the line of stones, eyes fixed on the entrance that seemed more like the wide mouth of a deadly cave now. His toes dug desperately into the ground beneath, until they cramped up.

It was precisely this moment Yvellios would never forget. When his chest began to burn and he could not allow himself to inhale. When breathing was an essential part of time passing.

The shock, as a man emerged from behind the door frame and stumbled into the front yard, got his knees collapsing. He fell back into the yellow bed of his mother's laboriously grown flowers. The man stared at him with eyes wide open. The linen sack in his hand seemed to contain a heavy filling. Just light enough to be held with one hand. So he could hold a knife in the other. A shiny elvish blade.

Yvellios expected a lot of things to happen. The loudest image his mind drew was the blade buried in his flesh with only one outcome to expect.

But instead, the stranger hurried away. His body moved too fast for his left foot to follow. If he had jumped to his feet just then, Yvelllios would have had a chance to get his hands on the stolen valuables. The stolen knife. His father's.

But he remained.

Metal clanking followed the man's path. Yvellios buried his fingers in the cold earth and clung to it. The trees behind their house swallowed the thief, while Yvellios kept staring at the spot he had just vanished from.

It was another groan that sent him back to reality. The world was moving faster. Too fast for his consciousness to process. One moment his fingers were digging into the damp earth. The next, they were gripping his mother's arm.

She was lying on the wooden floor. Next to the old cupboard, once filled with elvish necklaces, bracelets and a few jugs. A red spot spread on her white apron. It had its origin in a spot on her belly. Yvellios could not see it. Her hand kept it covered.

"Yve," she gasped, reaching for his cheek. Smiling with watery eyes.

"Mama." The word barely had a sound.

Yvellios felt his face turn into a grimace, saw his mother's become paler each second and he wasn't able to control any of it. There was only red. On her clothes. On the floor. On his hands, as he tore on her apron.

Her already cold hand grabbed his head, and he was pressed against her chest.

"No, I can heal you!" he cried and released himself from her weak grip. "I can heal you!" With both his shaking palms on her belly, Yvellios pinched his eyes tight.

It will work! It will work! It will work!

He hummed her song and waited for the warmth to fill his fingertips. Waited and waited.

It will work! It will! It will! It will!

When he opened his eyes and his vision spun from exhaustion, both hands remained unchanged. And so did the wound. He stared at the scene.

His mother reached for him again. "Yve, it's okay," she whispered.

Throwing himself into her limp arms, he cried out as he realized. "I'm sorry!"

"No. No. Don't be."

"I'm so sorry! I'm so sorry!"

"Yve. I love you." He continued weeping into her hair, his arms wrapped around her neck. His mother's hand slowly stroked his back for a while. Until the last stroke went down his back and ended on the wooden floor.

Home had become an unbearable silent prison. Yvellios stared at the dirty wooden piles in the kitchen area, until he was sure her body would appear again any second. He still saw the body. A corpse, resembling nothing his mother had been.

She's dead, Yvellios thought and felt nothing.

Everything she had brought into this world seemed to be further devoured with every hour of her absence. Including him.

He pressed the hand she held just a few days ago against his chest. His palm was still full of her touch. And now, there was nothing.

Nothing in his hand, nothing at home, nothing in his heart.

How could nothing be yet so hurtful?

From outside the house, distant chatter approached. Yvellios froze, for he knew the voices all too well.

"They said, they found him sleeping on her body."

"And there was blood on him. Everywhere!"

"You think it was him?"

"Maybe. Could be. I wouldn't be surprised."

Three figures appeared in the window frame. "You were right! You were right! He's still here!"

"Told you." The boys gathered at the open window and pushed each other, desperate for a perfect glance at what was presented inside.

"Oh my god. Look at him!"

"The door is unlocked!"

Yvellios pressed his elbows to his knees and covered his head. He knew what was to come.

"It smells worse than dog shit in here!"

"Ew, I bet it's him. Look at that!"

"Disgusting."

Yvellios kept his head low. They were all around him now.

"Ey!" One of them pushed him to the side. "What's it with you? You forgot how to bathe?" Finally, Yvellios raised his eyes to meet the ones glaring down on him. He had never seen them from another angle. "First, you had no father to teach you manners and now that your mother's dead, you can't even clean yourself?"

One of them laughed. "Maybe we should help him?"

"Yeah, let's get him to the river!" The others agreed.

"Don't touch me," Yvellios whispered as two of them tried to grab his arms. He pushed them away with all the strength he had left. It wasn't much but caught them off guard. "Leave me alone!"

They exchanged glances. "Take his arms."

Yvellios backed away. With his feet kicking the air, he kept them at a distance for a while, until they got hold of his ankles. His swollen eyelids turned hot again. "No! Stop! Stop it!" he screamed.

With nothing to hold on to, they dragged him across the floor and through the door onto the front yard. He was never considered strong. He was never considered a threat. Maybe that's why he had been so irrelevant all along. Stones scratched through the back of his shirt as they kept pulling, but all he felt was the ever-growing rage.

Yvellios reached for the boy's ankle to his right. Although he gained nothing but pitiful laughter and a bruised finger, he reached again. This time with success. Without hesitation, he bit into the back of his foot, just above the heel.

"Aah! He's going crazy!" There was no blood. Nevertheless, both hands let go of him. They backed away. Terrified.

One boy, the bitten one, made a furious attempt to get hold of Yvellios again. But he jumped to his feet and ran.

They followed for a while. However, Yvellios's anger was a better fuel. He didn't remember when they lost him, or the dirty words fell silent. It wasn't about them anymore.

Yvellios ran until his bare feet burned. Until his face turned wet and salty, covered in sweat and tears. Until he couldn't feel his legs and the pain in his soles was just something he carried along. Until his vision blurred, and he had no recognition of his surroundings. Until finally, he tripped and fell.

"Oh, my dear! You wanna ruin that beautiful face?" Yvellios didn't know where that voice came from. In his dizziness, he barely managed to push himself onto his knees.

A pair of dirty brown boots appeared in front of him. He looked up and saw a tall, slender man in gorgeous, multi-layered green robes. In the middle of his dazzling grin, two even lines of white teeth stood out. Pale skin nestled around his soft facial features. Two light green eyes shone against the contrast of his dark brown hair, tied up into a messy half bun. Apart from his slightly tired expression, he looked like a living and walking sculpture.

Yvellios imagined how magnificent the robes would flaunt in a light breeze.

The man bowed and held out his hand to Yvellios, who was still half-lying on the ground. "Wanna get up?" Now on eye-side, Yvellios not only noticed the man's weird sour smell, but also his pointy ears. His mouth popped open but froze before a word was formed. Never before had he met another one.

As the elf realized Yvellios would not stand up, he lifted his robes with a heavy sigh and settled down as well. He then reached behind him and brought out a lute, which was laced to his back with a leather strap around his chest.

Yvellios thought he'd throw up.

"Wanna hear a song?" the elf asked.

No!

"I usually don't give private performances, but you know what?" He grinned and winked. "For you I'll make an exception."

The stranger played his song before Yvellios could think of refusing. It was a cheerful melody, which he almost did not recognize. As the elf started to sing, he seemed to breathe the verses and live from them. The lute's melody melted with his singing and together they created a honey sweet noise. When he finished, Yvellio's heart felt it would shatter his ribcage any moment. His mother never sang this song accompanied by an instrument.

"The last verse was wrong," he said quietly.

A strange expression appeared on the elf's face for a moment, but he laughed it off. "Such a bitter child. You want to teach me your version? I would be pleased!"

Yvellios shook his head. "It's my mother's song."

"Well, not to be rude, but you look pretty lost. How about I walk you home and she teaches me the right lines?" the elf suggested and winked again.

"She's dead," Yvellios said out loud for the first time. He was waiting for his body's reaction. Tears maybe? But the rage was gone and now there was nothing.

The elf bit his lips. Then he said with a warm smile: "What a shame, I really would've loved to hear her sing."

Me too. But she was dead. And so were her songs.

The man let his elegant fingers glide over the strings once more. Slow, deep chords merged into a high staccato, leading to the familiar melody all over again.

Yvellios stared at him, and the elf stared back. He wanted to open his mouth. To sing the verse he loved so much. But there was nothing. He wanted the words to float on his tongue as they always did. He would have even spat them out if he could. But there was nothing but tears on his face.

When the music stopped, Yvellios dried his wet face with the dirty sleeves of his shirt. The now brown-red strained shirt he had not changed yet.

He heard a dull sound before two arms wrapped around him. Enclosed in a tight embrace his face was pressed against the stranger's shoulder. Slowly his hands grabbed into the robe's fabric gluing his body to the elf's. The sobbing began shortly after, covering the probably expensive fabric in salt water and gooey slime. Even though the man's sour smell was hard to bear, Yvellios felt his lungs fully grasp air again.

They crouched like this until Yvellios's breath calmed and he lifted his head.

"Promise you'll take care," the elf said as he reached for the lute and got back up. On both his feet, he suddenly opened his eyes and blinked twice. He had never seen someone blink so vigorously. "Uh, that was too fast." He then used his hands to shield his eyes. Yvellios couldn't make out what he shielded them from. "Believe me when I tell you, the effects of some pleasures are not worth their good time."

He did not fully understand what he meant, but he thought he understood enough. Yvellios reached for the man's sleeve. Slightly confused, he let the boy take his hand. With both his palms surrounding the cold and sweaty one Yvellios hummed the song. A weak attempt, which ended in nothing but hoarse noises. If it weren't for the melody, curing a headache demanded a simple spell. Finally, the elf's eyes lit up.

"Wow," he laughed. "That makes you the most useful child I ever met my entire life!" Yvellios looked down. If the man knew, he would probably take that back.

"I'll be playing some songs at The Bedry tomorrow." Noticing Yvellios puzzled expression he added with a laugh: "A tavern. If you come along, I can have Mildred make you some soup and you just listen. Or you sing along. It's usually quite busy, so no one will understand whatever you say." He winked once more and grinned. "Alright!" He bowed lightly. "It was the greatest pleasure for me to make your acquaintance, Sir!"

Against all expectations, the corners of Yvellios's lip went up.

With the lute on his back and a smile on his lips, the elf tousled Yvellios's hair before he headed down the road in an elegant yet carefree gait. The robe flaunted just as Yvellios imagined.

With every step the elf took away, Yvellios was left with less and less. The smile vanished first. Only the weight on his chest remained until the end.

"Take me with you," his mouth brought forth. Lips whispering what his mind screamed. Even though he considered his voice too quiet for the man to hear, he stood still abruptly.

"Please! I want to hear you play again. There is no one else…" He stopped as his throat blocked the words from rushing out. "Please. Take me with you!" he demanded with more confidence, because otherwise he'd have to return to nothingness. To where it was just him and the dirty piles.

Because, when the elf sang his song, there was nothing but the music.

And the music was more. It was more than nothing.

Isabel Harry is a fantasy writer dedicated to delivering readers with compelling characters and richly developed worlds. Originally from London, she now spends her days ghostwriting, guest blogging, and polishing up her debut fantasy novel. When she's not hard at work on her laptop, she can be found traveling the globe in search of new inspiration.

Instagram: @isabel_writing

A Fate Unwritten
by Isabel Harry

The wind blew into me, snaking into my clothes and bringing a red flush to my cheeks. Yet I smiled. After five days hunched over a desk, the weekend could not have come sooner. I tried to set thoughts of my job aside, but the monotony of my week weighed on me. My current job could not be all there was for me. I only wished someone would tell me what to do.

Shaking my head, I continued my walk to the library. When I reached its doors, I was greeted by the familiar warm embrace of hundreds of books. The contented silence of the people within enveloped me. This was my happy place.

I began to walk the shelves, running my hands over thrillers and cookbooks, romance novels and fantasy adventures. I knew this place like the back of my hand. These aisles were my escape.

But as my eyes drifted across the shelves, I saw a book I had not seen before. The fabric spine was wrought in dazzling patterns of white and gold, and I couldn't help but draw in a breath. Those were my favourite colours. Entranced, I delicately picked up the book and turned the first page.

'Our story begins in a London hospital room, where a baby was brought into the world. This baby did not have a father, at least not one she would ever know. It would be her mother who raised her, bleeding out funds from her struggling coffee shop to support this child and her four siblings. Yet despite her dire childhood, this baby would go on to do unimaginable things. She would change the world.'

I do not know for how long I stood there. I consumed the words as if I needed them to live, and a story unravelled itself inside my mind. I read of a girl who was bullied and poor. I read as she spent all her time studying, doing everything she could to bring herself out of the life she hated. I read as she moved away from home and began an office job—a job she grew to despise.

I was reading the story of my life.

Soon, the events of the book caught up to the present. My heart began to race. With shaking fingers, I flipped to the next page. This was the page that would detail my future.

It was blank.

I could not move. My gaze was paralysed on the empty page before me, as if staring at it could bring words into being. I would change the world, it had said. I needed to know how. There had to be another copy of this book somewhere, a completed copy that could give me my answers. And so I vowed, then and there, that I would find it.

Yet before I left, I did what I had feared to do. I turned to the front of the book and read the title.

'Naomi James'

It was my name.

I took the next week off work, and I scoured the internet for any mention of the book. Food lay uneaten in my fridge, and my small apartment grew messy and unkempt. I called every known library on the face of the earth to no avail. Yet as I dangled on the verge of failure, I heard the muffled ping of my computer. An email.

'Thank you for your inquiry to the Beijing Hidden Library, I believe we have what you seek.'

I did not waste another minute. By morning, I had blindly stuffed a bag and was boarding a plane to Beijing. I had spent my entire savings on this flight, but I did not regret it. This was it; I would finally have my answers.

Once in Beijing, I followed the maze of streets. My heart beat in time with my quickened footsteps, and before long, I was standing outside a grimy restaurant. Dread weaved its way through my gut. I had been duped. This was no library. My life savings were gone, and I was no closer to understanding my future.

Then a woman stepped from the restaurant. She was small and frail, but her eyes were full of energy. "You must be Naomi," she accented softly. My heart shuddered to a stop, and I nodded, unable to speak as I followed her into the restaurant.

She led me through the restaurant's back door, revealing a musty room bathed in grey. I gasped. Piles of books towered around me, reaching like paper skyscrapers to the ceiling. I noticed dust coating their spines, and I wondered if these books had ever been read.

I turned back to the woman behind me and saw she was holding a book of her own. It was tattered and greyed over with dust, but I still recognised it. It was my book.

She handed it to me. My heart leapt to my throat as I returned to the page I had left off at. Gingerly, I flipped it.

It was blank.

I flipped to the next one.

Blank.

Again and again, I turned the pages. All of them were blank. This couldn't be happening. Tears sprung to my eyes as I hopelessly flicked the last page. I stopped breathing.

'On April 1st, 2023, Naomi James will die.'

My eyes shot to the woman before me. That was today's date.

Before I could speak, my throat began to constrict. My hands shot to my neck, and within seconds, I was wheezing and choking. I stared wildly at the woman in front of me, but her eyes were pools of calm.

"We are not meant to know our futures, Naomi James," she said, "that book was a temptation, meant only to test you. You have failed, and now you must die."

Gasping for breath, I fell to my knees. The book tumbled to the floor. My vision began to blur as death descended upon me. Above, the woman gave a pitying smile.

In the last seconds of my life, something came over me. Without a thought, my hands flew from my neck, grabbing the book from the ground. I was desperate; I was dying. This was my last chance.

I ripped the last page from the book—the page foretelling my death. The sound of the tearing paper echoed as a scream about the room. It was the sound of a woman changing her fate, and it was terrifying.

Slowly, my airways began to open. I sat on the ground, panting the life back into me. Eventually, I made my eyes meet the woman looming above me. Her face was shrouded in the jagged shadows cast by the books around her, but I did not miss the shock in her eyes. Nor the respect.

After many more minutes, she let me leave.

I returned home.

Once I arrived, I quit my job. I was done with waiting for somebody else to tell me my future. I knew now the rest of my story was not for me to find; it was for me to write. So I decided to begin a charity, and I worked on helping young girls empower their future.

I believe I changed the world.

DID YOU KNOW?

Reading Makes You Happier!

"Since a good book can work wonders in alleviating stress and depression, it's pretty obvious why people who read more are more self-confident and happy.

By surveying more than 4,000 adults, the University of Liverpool concluded that readers are happier, less stressed, cope better with challenges, and have more close friends than non-readers. Isn't that a fun fact about reading? (pun by all means intended)"

From: https://basmo.app/facts-about-reading/

Resources

Find the Freelancer You and Your Book Need

Artists/Designers

Daphne Paige

Instagram: @daphne.paige.books
Instagram: @popcorn_publishing

I love illustrating book covers for other indie authors, as well as digital pieces of their characters which can be used for commercial purposes, such as stickers or prints.

I create character illustrations for book covers and marketing material with a specialty in the fantasy genre.

Instagram: @CaffeinateArt
Website: www.natephilbrick.com

CaffeinateArt

Angela Patera

I offer art for book covers and general illustration work to interested authors. Being a writer myself, I believe I might be the right person to bring your ideas to life on a canvas. I'm a self-taught artist who creates fantasy, science-fiction, horror, and nature-inspired art, but I'm open to anything.

Both Instagram and Twitter: @angela_art13

Rachel Meyer Freelance

Do you need help writing emails, blog posts, or web pages to promote your book or author business? I can help. I'm a copywriter specializing in e-commerce and a novelist myself. You get more time for writing while I handle all the hard copywriting work. Plus, my background as a novelist helps me understand your work like no other copywriter.

Website: https://rachelmeyerfreelance.
wixsite.com/copywriter/home

Mayonaka Designs

I provide an extensive choice of design services such as book cover designs, interior formatting, and social media graphics to help turn my clients' visions into realities.

Instagram: @mayonaka.designs
Carrd: https://mayonakadesigns.carrd.co/

Arash Jahani Book Design/Covers

I'm Arash, a book designer, and illustrator living in Florida. If you're Looking for an experienced book designer, I am here to help with all of your needs. My goal as a designer is to provide high-quality work for budgets both big or small, while always keeping my client's passion and feedback in mind.

Instagram: @bookcover.designer
Website: https://arashjahani.com/

Sakura Artist

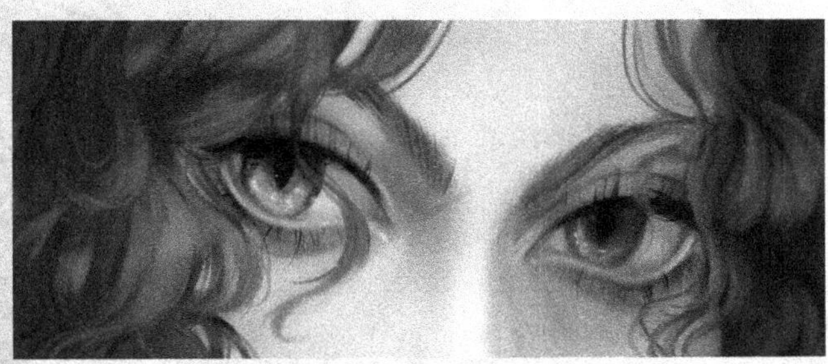

Amelia • 28 • Freelance Illustrator
Co-Creator of @ahcomicmagic
Illustrator for 'The Safekeepers' on Webtoons

Website: https://linktr.ee/Sakuraartist
Instagram: @sakuraartist

MoonPress Design

Hello! I'm Bianca and I'm a book cover designer based in Atlanta, GA. As a professional cover designer, I've been able to work with bestselling authors, publishing houses and indie authors on a variety of different projects and genres. Being able to connect and work with professionals in the writing industry is one of the best parts of the cover design business! I specialize in creating designs for covers that meet their expectations as well as the current market standard.

Instagram: bookcover.designer
Website: https://arashjahani.com/

Small Press/Publications

Winter Forest Press

Winter Forest Press publishes mystery, science fiction, and dystopian books.
Our debut publication, A Rogue Game, is coming in 2023.
While we are not currently accepting manuscript submissions, we may in the future. Sign up to get the latest updates.

Website: https://www.winterforestpress.com/
Instagram: @winterforestpress

Azala Press

This small publishing house was founded by author @mkahearn. books and specializes in themed fantasy anthology books.
See their website for submission opportunities along with their previously published works.

Website: https://azalapress.com/
Instagram: @azalapress

Smacked

Smacked is a monthly multimedia zine edited by Hunter Schmuck. Its aim is to provide creatives an outlet that is independently maintained. Though Smacked focuses on local work, the publication also provides a platform for anyone in the world who chooses to send in work. Each edition is available for free both digitally and in a limited physical edition. The freedom of the zine format allows for each issue to be whatever it needs to be—whether that means crazy formatting, uncanny art features, and/or a lack of artistic censorship.

Submit to: smackedzine@gmail.com
Instagram: @smackedzine

Quill and Flame Publishers

If you've got a YA or NA (your protagonists are 13-18 or 18-early twenties respectively) story that has a cracking plot, swoony romance, and characters you'd literally die for, we want to read it!

Website: https://quillandflame.com/
Instagram: @quill.and.flame.publishers

SnowRidge Press

SnowRidge Press has one goal: helping you achieve success. Founded by two self-published authors, we know the unique challenges that come with publishing. We're here to help and guide you through every step of the publishing journey. We charge less for our services because we know that most indie authors have less to spend. It's a choice we make every day to make editing, formatting, and publication services more accessible to everyone, because more good books in the world is always a good thing.

Website: https://snowridgepress.com/
Instagram: @snowridepress

Editors

Hunt Editorial

HuntEditorial.HE@gmail.com
Instagram: @Hunt.Editorial

Hunt Editorial - provides editing services for Authors and Aspiring Authors with regards to Developmental Editing, Copy /Line Editing, Mechanical Editing and Proofreading. At an affordable price while also offering payment plans for those who find themselves on a tight budget. Aiming to provide a great service that uplifts authors and their work as well as giving them a support system in their journey. Turning their Manuscript into a Masterpiece.

Denica McCall Editing

I provide manuscript evaluations, copyediting, and proofreading services for authors, specializing in YA fiction.

www.denicamccall.com
Instagram: @denicamcauthor

Sera Amoroso

Instragram: @seraamoroso

I provide editorial services for authors that is offered as an alternate, cheaper route to professional editing. As I am a student editor, all of my prices will be cheaper than market price and will remain that way until I receive my master's degree. The editing services I provide are as follows: developmental editing, copy editing, line editing, and proof reading. If you're interested, get a quote today!

Wisteria Editing

We offer inexpensive and efficient editing, customizable for each individual. This includes everything from developmental to proofreading.

https://wisteriaediting.com/home

Editor H. A. Pruitt

Website contact page:
https://www.hapruitt.com/contact

I provide editing services for authors working on their manuscripts. For $0.008 per word, I provide developmental editing, content editing, copyediting, and proofreading (two rounds of editing). I am open to all genres except horror and erotica, and I am open to hard topics but will not accept manuscripts with excessive cursing, sexual content, or gore. If you have any questions, please ask.

Jon Tilton's Editing Services

Editing that will take your writing to the next level! Jon doesn't just edit your work, he also explains the "why" behind his suggestions. His notes are more than a simple list of changes—they're also a guide to improve your writing, tailored to your personal strengths and weaknesses. As an independent author himself, Jon understands your need to make every dollar count. You will receive detailed notes covering your manuscript from every angle. Each edit also includes optional phone time to discuss your work. FREE sample edit available upon request. Book your next developmental or line edit today!

Website: www.jontilton.com/editing

Mendell Studios

I. Love. What. I. Do. Working with authors to help them bring their stories to life is a true joy— and I do my very best to ensure that my authors feel my joy throughout the project!
Not only will you have my utmost respect, commitment to the craft of writing, technical prowess, and extensive expertise in character development, but you'll have a new friend with whom you'll complete the journey. Let's write together!
Editor & Copywriter || fantasy, Christian fiction, and nonfiction/theology || Developmental edits || Line & copy edits|| Theological development

Website: www.mendellstudios.com
Instagram: @mendellstudios

Promotionals

The Godsend Backfire by Harold Straugh

Take a trip through time with Roldian, a Nephillim, sent down to earth to protect humans from his brothers. His brothers, one being the original vampire and the other being the original werewolf, are terrorizing Earth. Over the span of three books, Roldian turns into more of monster than his brothers.

You can find The Godsend Backfire on Amazon

Once Upon Her Veins by Rachael Katharine Elliott

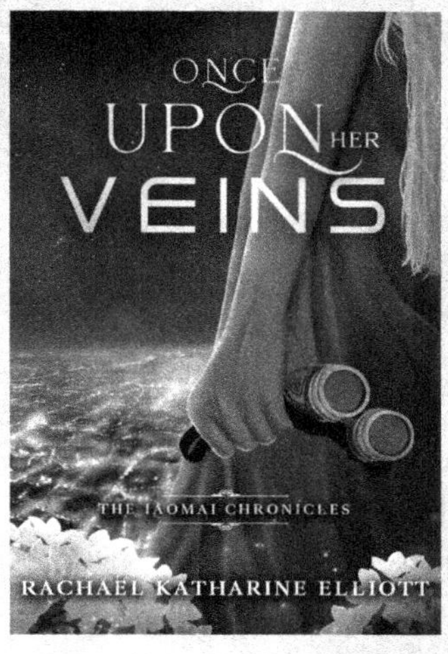

Mzia is a village healer in an empire crumbling from years of drug wars and unrelenting illnesses. But her blood harbors a dangerous secret, and with it, she fights to bring balance back to her broken world. When she is kidnapped by the very government that wants her silenced, Mzia is forced to ally herself with sworn enemies, question dearly held beliefs, and choose what she is willing to sacrifice to keep the truth alive.

Instagram: @catching_stardust
Website: rachaelkelliott.com
You can find Once Upon Her Veins on Amazon

Taking Flight by Careena Campbell

Princess Lovanna should be thrilled to be engaged to Prince Ryker, but something in her soul doesn't feel right. She's spent so long building a facade of who she thinks she should be, she's lost sight of who she actually is. What if she ends up trapped in a marriage with someone who loves a version of her that isn't real. Meanwhile, Lovanna's best friend, the dragon princess Sapphira, is afraid her inability to fly will discourage any dragons from ever being interested in her. In this heartwarming tale, both princesses must learn to embrace how God created them before it's too late.

Instagram and YouTube: @careenas_adventures
You can find Taking Flight on Amazon

The Hidden Library & Society Secrets Book One by Elsa Singer

When the Reed family move to Utah, where Robin's Dad had grown up, he didn't expect the adventures that he now faces about every month. In the first two installments of the series, he makes three friends, Nicole, Jess and Jaiden who help him capture El Duende and with the help of his science teacher, Thomas Smith, they defeat a lake monster and meet a peculiar woman from Thomas's past.

Society Secrets Book 1 - After his dad died, Kurt Reynolds doesn't feel fit filling in his shoes, despite the fact he feels obligated to, being the only boy in the family. After pulling one too many pranks at his highschool, he is sent to the capital city to attend their military school. While there, he meets his four team members and three adult triplets who all try to stop the Rebels Against their nations Republic from obtaining the most powerful stone in the universe.

Instagram: @elsas.galacticvoyages
You can find Elsa Singer's books on Amazon

A Sky of Tragic Moons Anthology

The universe is full of life.
Life is full of sorrow.
There are beings who walk between the stars, longing for love.
There are rebels fighting for freedom.
There are museums dedicated to all that has been lost.
There are humans dying so that others can survive.
The universe is full of life,
not all life is meant for the universe.

You can find A Sky of Tragic Moons on Amazon

Greentale Mysteries: The Last Guardian by Jackie Marie

Amanda Green just wanted to be an ordinary teenager and enjoy her summer vacation with her friends, but when her brother stops by to visit her at her new job everything changes. What happens next opens up a whole new world for her. Will she rise to the occasion and fulfill her destiny or will she turn her back on fate?

Instagram: @jackiemariebooks
You can find Greentale Mysteries on Amazon

This is Noir Series by AudraKate Gonzalez

Noir exists everywhere, and in every Noir weird stuff is always happening. Ghosts, monsters, ghouls, and more reside there. The destination is set, so travel across the states for chills, thrills, and things that go bump in the night...

Instagram: @lets.get.lit.erature
Website: www.authoraudrakategonzalez.com

The Curse of Ragoh
by Kate Korsak

Conroy Roan, the youngest prince of Ragoh, dreams of fire. Every night, flames dance across his vision and smoke fills his lungs, but every night he wakes up. They are just dreams, after all. Until one night, he doesn't. One night, the dreams became reality, and Conroy loses everyone and everything he once loved. As Conroy digs deeper into the fire, he comes face to face with the Curses of Akinar, and The Fae that once worked with his kingdom will stop at nothing to get their freedom. Freedom that only he, the last heir of Roan, can grant.

You can find The Curse of Ragoh on Amazon and Kindle

The Archives of Icínq-Régn, Books One-Five
by Garrett K. Jones

Do you enjoy dragons? How about elves? What about Magic, and vampires that DON'T sparkle?!? If so you're going to love the adventures taking place throughout Icínq-Régn - the Five Kingdoms. The downfall of a despot warlord kickstarts a series of grand adventures spanning two generations of characters. Start your quest with "The Heirs of Menonias", learn about "The Destiny of Dragons", see the "Rise of the Shadowkin", meet "Hadran Corvis of Farfell", and explore "The Mantle of the Farherless". All titles available today!!!

Website: www.archivesofthefivekingdoms.com/books

Pale Phoenix
by Noah Lynch

Wolfram's memory is gone, but his past sins and the mob that he served are not. Will he choose to become a better man, or return to the sinful, blood-soaked life that leads only to death? Judas Shapiro never meant to get tangled up in a world of intrigue and mob violence. Is his only hope this mysterious stranger who seems to have more ties to the mob than Judas is comfortable with? Witness a tale of redemption, consequences, manipulation, love, guilt, and change in Pale Phoenix. Available on Paperback and Kindle on Amazon from Noah Lynch

Instagram: @silverhandpublishing
You can find Pale Phoenix on Amazon and Kindle

Please Return to the Lands of Luxury by Jon Tilton

Embark on a thrilling adventure with Jane and her friends. Filled with dynamic characters and robot action, this heart-warming tale will delight readers of all ages. Please Return to the Lands of Luxury is the first book in this exciting, new series, packed with an abundance of adventure, plenty of heart, and timeless themes. Available in paperback, hardback, audiobook, and on Kindle!

Website: www.jontilton.com
You can find the Lands of Luxury on Amazon and Barnes & Noble

The Makria Cycle: Torsion and Clandestine by Sera Amoroso

The Makria Cycle is a science fiction trilogy geared towards ages 13-25. It follows the story of nine people who get accepted into a STEM based college and unwittingly join an experiment. They will overcome obstacles, uncover secrets, and face themselves and their ideals. Chock full of espionage, science, aliens, found family fun, and family fun. So, if you love scifi, relate to tired college students, or just want to find out what happens next, go ahead and pick up a copy of Torsion and Clandestine.

Website: https://seraamoroso.wixsite.com/seraamoroso/

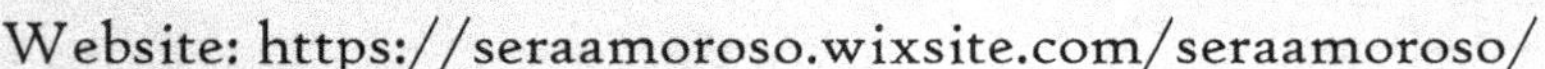

In Touch by Valerie Parente

Undergraduate student Jef meets an obsessive compulsive student Lacey in this realistic fiction novel. Throughout a school year these two exchange ideas that merge science with art, reality with fantasy, and physical phenomena with mental phenomena. While learning from one another Jef makes it his mission to make sense of Lacey's nonsensical disorder and all of its incredible ironies; how she lives to feel everything emotionally but dreads feeling anything physically, how her mind lives to protect as it gradually wreaks destruction, and most paradoxically how both Lacey's most rewarding qualities and most detrimental flaws manifest from the same brain.

Website: www.valerieparente.com
You can also find In Touch on Amazon

Bleached Reminders
by Effie Joe Stock

A mini, spooky anthology collection for lovers of both animals and bones, Bleached Reminders will leave you contemplating the finality of death while also comforted by the warm love of beloved animals.

Each piece in this anthology holds a bit of fantasy and a bit of truth, along with a very gentle whisper to remind you that you are never truly alone, not even when faced with death.

Instagram: @effie.joe.stock.author
Website: www.effiejoestock.com
You can also find Bleached Reminders on Amazon

Unexpected Encounters of a Draconic Kind and Other Stories
by Beka Gremikova

Encounters. Whether with magic or science, whether expected or unexpected, they can change our minds, our destinies...even our world. In this collection of twenty-two short stories, journey alongside a mother determined to provide for her family in perilous jungles; an auntie facing off against a disgruntled house spirit; a young half-human, half-mermaid girl on the search for her father with murderous soldiers on her heels; and many more. From comedy to mystery to thriller, these stories will be an encounter that just might change you.

Instagram: @beka.gremikova
Website: www.bekagremikova.com
You can also find Beka Gremikova's Works on Amazon and SnowRidge Press

Aphotic Love
by Dragon Bone Publishing

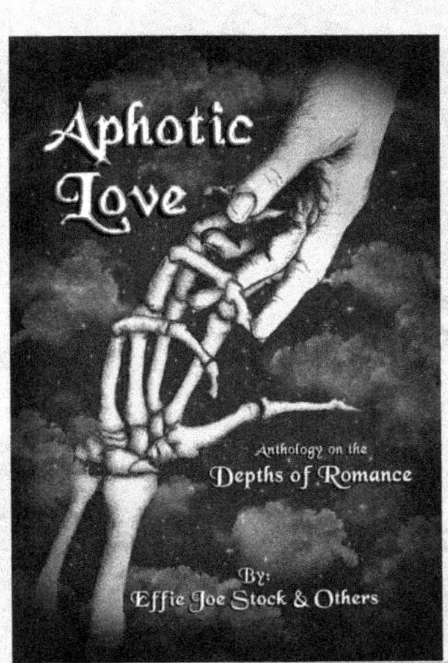

Aphotic: devoid of light, a depth beyond comprehension.
Love, often depicted as light, joyful, fun, exciting, carefree, also a darker side—a deeper, frightening, desperate, tragic side.
Dare to dive deep into this raw, emotional collection of short stories, prose, and poems which strives to expose the lightless side of tragedy, heartbreak, desperation, and love.

Website: www.dragonbonepublishing.com
You can also find Aphotic Love on Amazon

The Sun Still Rises
by Cassandra Hamm

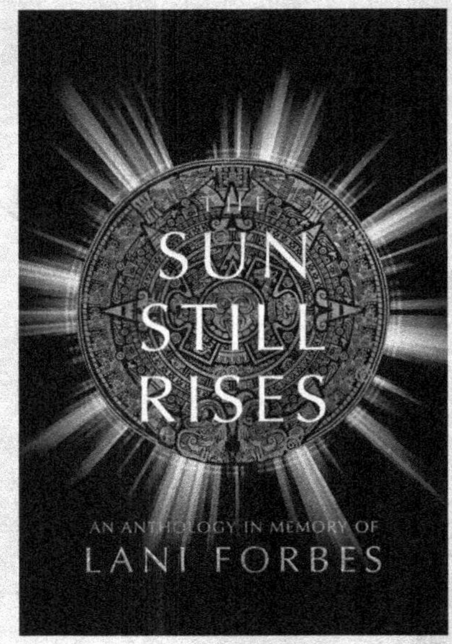

Light shines brightest in dark places... A selfish empress slowly turns to gold. A highschooler's hallucinations reveal a dangerous new world of Faerie. An outcast battles shadow demons to save her people from plague. This charity collection of YA fantasy stories celebrates the light found in dark places, just as Lani Forbes once embodied having hope in difficult times. Her spirit shines on through these beautiful, bittersweet tales full of fallen stars and fae princes, werewolves and magic wielders, samurai and smoky skies. Featuring stories from Ronie Kendig, Jill Williamson, Julie Hall, Carrie Anne Noble, S.D. Grimm, and more!

Instagram: @cassandrahammwrites
Website: https://www.cassandrahamm.com/
You can also find Cassandra Hamm's books on Amazon and Barnes & Noble

The Shadows of Light Series
by Effie Joe Stock

Child of the Dragon Prophecy is the first book in an epic fantasy series which follows Stephania, a Dragon Rider who's been raised amongst Centaurs and Humans and is the born savior of a Prophecy that isn't all it seems. Battling against losing her memories, an ancient magic that threatens to possess her, and a dangerous lyre that can control the forest, Stephania must decide if she'll let her past consume and destroy her, or if she'll embrace her destiny and rise to the Duvarharian throne.

Instagram: @effie.joe.stock.author
Website: www.effiejoestock.com
You can also find The Shadows of Light Series on Amazon

Traitors and Tyrants
by Stephanie Dunham

In a tale where resilience and self-discovery intertwine, Traitors & Tyrants, will captivate your imagination and leave you questioning the very essence of who we are and who we choose to become.

Rapunzel's suffocating captivity meets A Lust for Blood by K.C Smith, and Margaret Rogerson's, Vespertine, in this young adult dark high fantasy.

Instagram: @ authorstephaniedunham
Website: www.authorstephaniedunham.com